Only _____ to her family could _____ e dragged her to an alien world of drawing-rooms and scandalmongers...

As they strolled along beside the lake, Rod was not surprised when she turned to him and said, "I need your advice."

"I thought so. What is it?"

"It's Penny." She hesitated, her eyes cast down. "She is afraid that Jason is unfaithful. Could you possibly find out if he has a mistress?"

Rod fought to hide his consternation. "My dear Miss Kilmore, even if I were on sufficiently intimate terms with your brother, I could not discuss that subject. Though admittedly there are many men tasteless enough to gossip about their _chères amies_, I am not one of them."

"Oh! Then you have...?" Thea clapped her hands to her mouth, her face crimson, and Rod closed his eyes, appalled at where their mutual frankness had led him.

Regency England: 1811-1820

"It was the best of times,
it was the worst of times...."

As George III languished in madness, the pampered and profligate Prince of Wales led the land in revelry and the elegant Beau Brummel set the style. Across the Channel, Napoleon continued to plot against the English until his final exile to St. Helena. Across the Atlantic, America renewed hostilities with an old adversary, declaring war on Britain in 1812. At home, Society glittered, love matches abounded and poets such as Lord Byron flourished. It was a time of heroes and villains, a time of unrelenting charm and gaiety, when entire fortunes were won or lost on a turn of the dice and reputation was all. A dazzling period that left its mark on two continents and whose very name became a byword for elegance and romance.

Books by Carola Dunn

HARLEQUIN REGENCY ROMANCE
25—A SUSCEPTIBLE GENTLEMAN
39—A POOR RELATION
52—A LORD FOR MISS LARKIN
63—THE FORTUNE-HUNTERS
73—THE ROAD TO GRETNA
86—MY LORD WINTER

Don't miss any of our special offers. Write to us at the following address for information on our newest releases.

Harlequin Reader Service
P.O. Box 1397, Buffalo, NY 14240
Canadian address: P.O. Box 603,
Fort Erie, Ont. L2A 5X3

THEA'S MARQUIS
Carola Dunn

Harlequin Books

TORONTO • NEW YORK • LONDON
AMSTERDAM • PARIS • SYDNEY • HAMBURG
STOCKHOLM • ATHENS • TOKYO • MILAN
MADRID • WARSAW • BUDAPEST • AUCKLAND

Published May 1993

ISBN 0-373-31198-2

THEA'S MARQUIS

CHAPTER ONE

OUTSIDE THE CARRIAGE window, the October afternoon was fading fast. Inside, two of the passengers were doing likewise. Wan with exhaustion, Penny slumped back against the squabs, while Megan, a trifle green about the gills, moaned with the pain of a headache. Her bonnetless head was cradled in her mother's black bombazine lap, which was becoming positively damp from the trickle of tears Meg could not stop.

"Mama, we *cannot* go on as far as Stilton," Thea said with uncharacteristic determination. "I daresay it is another ten miles or more. Surely we shall come to another inn before then?"

"Your brother reserved rooms for us at The Bell," said the Dowager Lady Kilmore doubtfully.

"Jason will not mind where we stay. Penny, do you not think we ought to stop at the next inn?"

"Oh, please!" Meg cried out.

Their sister-in-law nodded without opening her eyes. "All I want is a bed, be it in a palace or a hedge-tavern."

"Mama?"

"Perhaps you are right, Thea. Tell Scargill to stop at the next inn, but only if it is respectable." She stroked her younger daughter's dark hair. "I know how miserably you feel, Meg darling, but truly you would not be comfortable in a hedge-tavern."

As she turned to open the sliding hatch to instruct the coachman, Thea saw Penny flush slightly at the dowager's gently indirect reproof. Dear Mama had no sense of humour, whereas Penny had a great deal, which made for frequent misunderstandings. Mama tended to suspect that her new daughter-in-law's odd utterances were due to her unfortunate background, and therefore to be tactfully corrected. Thea touched Penny's hand to show she knew her words had been ironic. Opening her grey-green eyes, Penny smiled at her gratefully.

After a brief exchange with Scargill, Thea turned back to the others. "He says this village is Wansford. There is a perfectly unexceptionable inn just ahead, so I told him we shall stay the night. The Haycock, it is called."

Penny started and looked out of the window, her cheeks flushing once again. In the dusk, Thea saw that the carriage was crossing a long bridge above a low-lying meadow, and then the twilight glinted on a placid river below. Nothing that she could see explained Penny's pink cheeks. No doubt something had happened during her ill-fated elopement, which had providentially ended in her marriage to Jason rather than her intended husband, Dr. Angus Knox. Thea resolved to ask her later, in private.

A moment later the carriage swung left and came to a halt in a courtyard surrounded by slate-roofed buildings of pale yellow stone. Three pairs of eyes turned towards Thea.

She quailed. Even where Jason had reserved rooms for them, she had found it difficult to walk into inns on the way south. Brought up on an isolated estate in the wilds of Northumberland, Thea was diffident with anyone but her family, and downright bashful with strangers.

Silently she castigated herself for a coward. It was up to her. Scargill was a countryman whose Northumberland dialect had already proved incomprehensible to those he disdained as foreigners. Besides, he was sadly rheumaticky and would complain bitterly about climbing down from the box. Under other circumstances, either Meg or Penny would have faced the most churlish of innkeepers without turning a hair, but Meg was unwell and Penny burnt to the socket. The Dowager Lady Kilmore, like her elder daughter, was uncomfortable with strangers. She was also inclined to an absentminded vagueness that made it unwise to leave arrangements to her.

Thea took a deep breath. Wishing she were six inches shorter, and that her threadbare blue woollen cloak were a modish velvet pelisse, she stepped down from the carriage.

An ostler approached from one side, a waiter with a white napkin over his arm from another. Rushing past them, Thea hurried into the inn.

The lobby, brightly lit by oil lamps hanging from the oak beams, was empty but for a few chairs standing against the whitewashed walls. On one side a door stood open to reveal a glimpse of a busy coffee-room, from which wafted appetizing odours. On the other side, rowdy voices and the smell of beer came from the taproom. Thea hesitated, dreading the thought of walking into either. She should have spoken to the waiter, she realized in dismay.

Then a stout, rubicund man in a blue coat with shiny brass buttons came out of the coffee-room. "What can I do for you, miss?" he enquired genially.

"We need rooms for tonight. Lady Kilmore and Lady...and the Dowager Lady Kilmore and two Misses Kilmore."

"I'm right sorry, miss, but you'll have to tell your mistress there's no room."

Thea blushed furiously, feeling dowdier than ever. "I...I am Miss Kilmore," she stammered.

"Begging your pardon, madam, I'm sure, but it don't make no difference. There was a mill today over to Collyweston and the house is full o' sporting gents. 'Tis only a matter o' six miles to Stamford, or nine to Stilton if so be you're going south. There's good enough inns both places."

"We cannot go farther. Please, we only need two chambers between us, or even one, if you have truckle beds."

The man looked harassed. "'Tis the truth, madam," he insisted, "I haven't a single chamber free."

"What's the trouble, Percival?" queried a deep, lazy voice. Down the stairs behind the innkeeper trod a large, fair-haired gentleman in elegant black evening clothes with a plain burgundy satin waistcoat. A ruby gleamed in the knot of his dazzlingly white cravat. Perfectly proportioned for his height, he was light on his feet, moving with the controlled grace of an active, vigorous man.

Percival swung round, spreading his hands in a gesture of helplessness. "My lord, this young lady wants rooms for the night and I simply don't have any."

Something in the gentleman's amiable face inspired confidence in Thea. "Sir," she cried, "my sister is wretchedly ill from the motion of the carriage and my sister-in-law is *enceinte*. They can go no farther tonight."

"Then they shall not, ma'am," he said calmly. "Do you not agree, Will?" Reaching the bottom of the stairs, the large gentleman moved aside.

From behind him emerged a slight figure in a purple coat, pale yellow pantaloons, and a waistcoat embroidered with purple, yellow-centred Michaelmas daisies. His light brown hair, cut in a fashionable Brutus, added an inch or two to his height, but when he had descended the last few steps Thea saw that his merry blue eyes were on a level with her own.

"I told you your foppery would make the ladies stare," the first gentleman continued, his deep voice amused.

Thea's cheeks grew hot. "I...I beg your pardon, sir," she faltered.

The young man laughed. "Not to worry, ma'am. A fellow likes to know his efforts are appreciated. What's going on, Rod? I couldn't hear a word through your Brobdingnagian bulk."

"Allow me, ma'am, to make known to you my cousin, William DeVine. I am Hazlewood. We shall be honoured if you will accept the use of our chambers for your ailing sisters."

"Here, I say, Rod!" protested Mr. DeVine. Then he caught a glance from Lord Hazlewood and resigned himself. "I mean, of course, ma'am, we shall be delighted to be of assistance." Drawing himself up to his full height, he turned to the landlord and ordered, "See to it, Percival."

"At once, sir, my lord." He bustled off, calling to his servants.

Lord Hazlewood brushed aside Thea's thanks with a smile. "I don't wish to hear another word on the subject, ma'am. Perhaps your invalids would be glad of support into the inn?'' he suggested with a gesture towards the door to the courtyard.

She led the way out into the chilly dusk. Towering at her side, he made her feel almost dainty despite her height. Mr. DeVine tagged along after them, grumbling to himself. Thea caught a few words: " ... Another of your damned quixotic quirks!'' The dandy was less than pleased to be cozened into giving up his chamber, but she could not feel guilty. Meg's and Penny's need was far greater.

Her mother was peering anxiously from the carriage door, her shabby black bonnet askew. She shrank back as she caught sight of Thea's stalwart companion.

"Mama, Lord Hazlewood will help Meg and Penny into the inn.''

"So will I,'' said Mr. DeVine indignantly, coming forward. "I may appear puny beside my titanic cousin but I hope I am strong enough to lend a lady my arm.''

Uncertain whether to apologize or to perform introductions, Thea hesitated.

Penny, decisive despite her fatigue, stepped down with the aid of Lord Hazlewood's hand. "Thank you, sir. I am Lady Kilmore.'' Though she sounded tired, after two months of marriage she was beginning to pronounce her title as if she believed in it, Thea noted. Leaning on his lordship's arm, she trudged wearily towards the inn.

Helped by her mother within, Mr. DeVine without, Meg next stumbled from the carriage, still hatless because her bonnet hurt her aching head. On either side of her woebegone face, dark curls escaped from plaited loops. Her small form shivered as the frosty air penetrated her cloak, which was as threadbare as Thea's.

"Will DeVine at your service, ma'am," said the young dandy with a gallant bow. He offered his arm.

She took it with a grateful glance and a pitiful attempt at a smile. "I am not in general so feeble, sir."

He had to bend his head to hear her faint murmur. With Meg beside him instead of his oversize cousin, he no longer appeared the least bit puny.

As Thea handed her mother down, the dowager whispered, "Who are these gentlemen, Thea? Surely you did not request assistance of strangers?"

She had not precisely *requested* assistance, she told herself guiltily. "They came into the hall when the innkeeper was telling me that he had no rooms available. Lord Hazlewood insisted on our accepting his and Mr. DeVine's bedchambers."

"How very kind." The elder Lady Kilmore's soft voice was full of doubt. "But a trifle odd, if you did not speak to him."

"I did speak to him, Mama," Thea confessed. "He asked the landlord what was the matter and I explained that Meg is ill and Penny increasing."

"Oh dear! It is most improper to mention that delicate subject to a gentleman, let alone to a complete stranger whom you ought not to have addressed at all."

Thea's heart sank. Lord Hazlewood probably considered her a shameless hussy. He must have been scandalized, though he was too chivalrous to let it show. "I did not think," she faltered. "I was worried about Penny."

"I fear I have not taught you well."

"Pray, Mama, do not blame yourself. Out of the world as we have been, I have had no chance to practise your lessons." Mortified, she entered the lobby with downcast eyes to avoid meeting his lordship's gaze.

To her relief, Mr. Percival took charge. The Kilmores were whisked upstairs. One chamber was already prepared, and on the opposite side of the passage a disapproving valet was just removing the last of his master's traps.

Meg and the dowager disappeared into the first room, followed by a mob-capped chambermaid wielding a warming pan. Thea waited with Penny outside the other chamber while the valet set down a monogrammed leather portmanteau in the passage and went back to check that he had left nothing behind. He came out reverently bearing a pair of glossy, gold-tasselled Hessians, picked up the portmanteau, and sailed past Thea and Penny with his nose in the air.

The room was large and luxurious, with a huge feather bed, a bow-fronted chest of drawers, and a mirror-fronted wardrobe. Before a cheerful fire stood a small table with two chairs. Penny sank onto one of the chairs and took off her stylish white-plumed bonnet, revealing flaming red hair.

"I wish Jason had come to fetch us." She sighed. "Sometimes I almost believe our marriage was a dream, only then I should not be pregnant and always out of curl. You don't think he left because he was already tired of me?" she added unhappily.

"Don't be a widgeon, Penny dear." Thea set her faded blue bonnet on the chest and crossed to the looking-glass to tidy coiled braids as dark as her sister's. "You know Jason had to go to London to look after your affairs and to make preparations for us to join him. From what he has written about the condition your uncle left your house in, I am surprised he has managed to make it fit to inhabit after so short a time."

Penny looked unconvinced, but the arrival of the chambermaid with the warming pan and hot water, and then a boy with their bags, put an end to confidences.

"Will your ladyship be wantin' any help?" asked the maid, adding with a hint of curiosity, "seein' as your abigail been't wi' you."

"Thank you, we shall help each other." Penny did not deign to provide an explanation for the lack of even a single abigail for four ladies.

Thea admired and envied her assurance. Only on the subject of Jason did Penny lose her self-possession. It was the wrong moment to ask about the connection of Wansford and The Haycock with her elopement. As Thea unpacked her sister-in-law's night shift and helped to unfasten her buttons, she talked of Lord Hazlewood and Mr. DeVine.

"Mama said I ought not to have spoken to them, and I have sunk myself beneath reproach by mentioning that you are with child, but I am glad I did since you and Meg can be comfortable."

"So am I! It was brave of you."

"Lord Hazlewood must suppose me shockingly coarse," Thea said wistfully, "yet he was so very kind and courteous. I only hope I never have to meet either of them again."

"Fustian!" Penny climbed into the high bed and sank back on the pillows with a sigh of relief. "They will put it down to your inexperience with the Polite World."

"If I were fresh from the schoolroom, perhaps, but I am five and twenty, past the age to be permitted a few *faux pas*. If it were not that you claim to need my support—which I don't believe for an instant!—I should refuse to make my bow to Society along with Meg." She tucked the counterpane around Penny. "I had best go and see how Meg and Mama go on. I shall return in a moment."

Meg, too, was already tucked up in bed. The sickly tinge had left her cheeks, though she was still pale. Their mother was bathing her forehead with lavender water to try to relieve the headache that still oppressed her.

"You will feel better when you have eaten something," said Thea comfortingly. "You hardly touched a bite at luncheon."

"If I had, I should have lost it long since," Meg pointed out with a flash of her usual spirit.

Someone tapped on the chamber door and Thea went to answer it. A tall, thin man dressed in sober black bowed to her respectfully.

"I am Pelham, madam, the marquis's gentleman. His lordship sends his compliments, and he begs the pleasure of the company of any of your party that's fit, to dine in his private parlour in an hour's time."

Dismayed, Thea started to refuse. "Oh, but we—"

"My daughter and I shall be happy to accept his lordship's kind invitation," interrupted her mother calmly, joining her by the door.

"My lady." The man bowed again and departed.

Thea closed the door and leaned against it, suddenly weak at the knees. "I thought they would have gone on to another inn. Mama, I cannot face Lord Hazlewood after behaving with such a lack of decorum."

"I fear you must, my love. Much as I dislike such intimacy with strangers, we cannot refuse without rudeness when he has been so excessively obliging."

"But he is a marquis!"

"And you are the daughter of a baron, Thea, not an ill-bred, discourteous nobody. Go and put on your blue silk. You and I shall dine with the marquis and Mr. DeVine."

CHAPTER TWO

THEA STARED AT HERSELF in the mirror, her dark eyes apprehensive. A plain white cambric spinster's cap hid her pinned-up braids, but Penny's skilful fingers had long since softened her once severely practical hairstyle. Now short curls adorned her brow and clustered at her temples.

That was the best part. Most of the colour was washed out of her best blue silk, and somehow its drooping shapelessness made her look even taller and thinner.

"I wish we had not decided to wait until we reach London before buying new clothes," she said despairingly. "I look like a scarecrow."

"Not even sackcloth could make you look anything but aristocratic," said Penny, somnolent after a nourishing bowl of thick, savoury beef-and-barley soup, followed by apple pie. "I'm taller than you by a good inch, but if I were as slender and fine-boned as you are, I should be *aux anges.*"

"Are you quite sure you do not mind being left alone?"

"Quite sure. I shall be asleep the moment you snuff the candles. Be off with you, Thea. Your marquis is less likely to take exception to your gown than to being kept waiting for his dinner."

Five minutes later, Mr. Percival himself ushered Thea and her mother into Lord Hazlewood's private parlour. A square table in the centre of the room was already set for four with spotless white linen and gleaming glasses. The gentlemen rose from their seats by the fire and made their bows. The marquis dwarfed the diminutive Lady Kilmore.

"I trust your invalids are on the mend, ma'am?" he enquired.

"Yes, indeed, they are both asleep already, thanks to your kindness." She paused, and Thea, her gaze fixed on her own clasped hands, was horridly afraid she was going to apologize for her elder daughter's misconduct. However, she merely went on in a vague way, "Such a tiresome journey."

"Are you bound for London, Miss Kilmore?" Mr. DeVine asked politely.

"Yes, sir." Venturing to peek at his face, Thea saw a flash of boredom, quickly hidden. She tried to think of something to say and failed.

"Are you acquainted with the city?" he struggled on.

"My sister and I have never been there. Megan is to make her come-out."

"You are going up for the Little Season, I expect," said Lord Hazlewood. "I commend your wisdom, Lady Kilmore. My mother took each of my sisters to Town in the autumn to learn how to go on in the world before diving into the maelstrom of the Season the following spring."

His calm voice gave Thea confidence. "That is part of it," she agreed. "Also, our home in Northumberland is often cut off by snow from December to March, or even April."

Mr. DeVine shuddered theatrically. "What a horrendous fate! No wonder you made your escape in good time."

"As I daresay you have already guessed from his dress, Will is a true Bond Street beau, never happy far from the metropolis," the marquis quizzed him.

"You malign me. Do not heed him, Miss Kilmore, it is envy speaks. Bond Street beaux are frippery fellows. *I* am a pink of the ton."

"Coxcomb," said his cousin as the door opened to admit a parade of waiters in striped waistcoats. Supervised by Mr. Percival, they bore in a steaming tureen, platters with pewter covers, casseroles and sauce-boats. Thea had never seen so many dishes served at once. She realized she was ravenous, but she had no intention of letting hunger overcome good manners. Mama should have no further cause to blush for her.

Even at home, with just the three of them, Lady Kilmore had always insisted that conversation was as important as food at the dinner table. Tasting the delicately flavoured *soupe à la reine,* Thea wondered whether to ask Mr. DeVine to explain the difference between a Bond Street beau and a pink of the ton. Nor was she precisely certain what a coxcomb was. Had they been unacceptable subjects for ladies, the gentlemen would not have spoken of them, but she did not want Lord Hazlewood to think her shockingly ignorant.

Before she could make up her mind, her mother asked if their host was travelling towards London or northward.

"We have just spent a few days at Hazlewood Castle, near York," the marquis said. "We are on our way to Town."

"Then you did not come to see the mill at Collyweston?" said Thea, recalling something that had puzzled her. "The landlord said he had no rooms available because there was a mill near here today. I do not understand how a mill could be there just for one day, nor why sporting gentlemen should go to see it."

"Percival referred to a pugilistic exercise, Miss Kilmore," explained Mr. DeVine, making a poor effort at hiding a grin.

She must have looked blank, for Lord Hazlewood frowned at his cousin and said kindly, "Will is flaunting his vocabulary, Miss Kilmore. He means a prizefight, a boxing match."

Judging by Mama's wrinkled forehead, *that* was no fit topic for a lady, but how could she have guessed? Once more she had blotted her copybook. "I thought he meant a windmill or a water-mill," she said, excusing herself miserably.

"A natural supposition," said the marquis. "The colloquial term is scarcely something a lady can be expected to know. I daresay Northumberland has many water-mills, Lady Kilmore? I am unacquainted with the county, but it is for the most part rough and hilly, is it not?"

Thea shot him a glance of fervent gratitude. She was beginning to think she would never dare open her mouth in company again, yet she felt she could say anything to Lord Hazlewood. If he was amused or shocked, he was by far too courteous ever to show it. She had dreaded meeting him again; now a faint hope raised its head that their paths might cross in London.

She finished her soup in subdued silence while the others talked about the beauty of the northern moors in summer, their bleakness in winter. Mr. DeVine oblig-

ingly helped her to some of the dishes before them. As
he consulted her taste before serving her, she was forced
to admit that several of the ragouts and sauces, and
even one or two vegetables, were unfamiliar to her.

"Percival sets an excellent table," he said, "which is
why Rod always stays here. My cousin calls himself a
gourmet, but the truth is, it takes a vast quantity of vi-
ands to keep up a man his size, and it would be dull
work stuffing himself with boiled beef and potatoes."

"Whereas Will starves himself for fear of spoiling the
set of his coat," retorted the marquis placidly. "Try
some of these quenelles, Miss Kilmore."

"What we plain folks call forcemeat dumplings," Mr.
DeVine informed her in a conspiratorial whisper. She
began to like him, and there was something most attractive about the affectionate way he and his cousin
teased each other.

By the time the table was cleared of dessert, Thea was
sufficiently at ease to wonder aloud what variety of
pears had been used to make a particularly delicious
tart. Mr. DeVine asked a waiter.

The man gaped at him. "I dunno, sir."

"Go and ask in the kitchen, man," he said impa-
tiently.

The waiter scurried off, while another set out tea for
the ladies and, with the ladies' permission, port for the
gentlemen. He had scarcely closed the door behind him
when it was flung open again and a small, plump man
in a chef's cap rushed in. Bowing with a flourish, he
beamed at Thea.

"Ah, *mademoiselle,* you are ze young lady zat de-
mands to know vat is zis *poire?* To you I kiss ze 'and.
Zese ozzer English, zey eat like pigs but nevair zey ask
ze intelligent qvestion. For zis *tarte aux poires,* I use

only ze Perkinson vordens. You add ze nutmeg, *un peu de gingembre*, cinnamon, and..." he looked around suspiciously, then muttered in her ear, "...and *un soupçon de poivre*. You are surprise, *hein?* Zis is mine secret."

Mr. DeVine was in fits of laughter. The Frenchman cast him a disdainful glance and bowed to the marquis. "Milord, you also appreciate ze art of *la cuisine*. Always Monsieur Percival, he tell me, '*Monsieur le Marquis* is here, do your best, Ambroise.' Ze dinner please you?"

"Excellent as always, Ambroise." Lord Hazlewood flipped a coin to the chef, who caught it with dexterity and dropped it into the pocket of his apron, where it clinked. Apparently other patrons enjoyed Ambroise's creations, if falling short of the true appreciation of the connoisseur.

He bowed to the flustered Lady Kilmore and strutted out.

"You have made a conquest, Miss Kilmore," said Mr. DeVine, smiling at her in a friendly way.

"What an odd man! If he knew how ignorant I am about cookery, he would not have told me his receipt."

"Do you mean to reveal the secret ingredient?" Lord Hazlewood asked. "He has never favoured me so highly."

Thea shook her head, feeling like a peagoose. "Even if I were prepared to betray his confidence, I fear I only understood one word in two, and I have no notion what the secret ingredient is."

The marquis and Mr. DeVine both laughed, but as if she had said something witty, not foolish.

"I shall have my chef experiment," said his lordship. "What kind of pears did Ambroise use?"

"Parkinson's wardens," Thea told him. "Wardens are good cooking pears, though too hard for eating. I have read of Parkinson's variety but never tried them. In the north—"

"Thea, if you have finished your tea it is time we retired," her mother interrupted, sounding anxious.

"Yes, Mama." What had she said wrong now? Once more abashed, she murmured her thanks to Lord Hazlewood for a delightful evening.

"It was our pleasure, ma'am. Lady Kilmore, I trust you will make use of this room when you break your fast tomorrow morning. Whether my cousin and I are about or not, you will be more comfortable than in the public coffee-room." He opened the door as he spoke and a hubbub of shouts, whoops, guffaws, and female squeals from that and the taproom met their ears.

The dowager assented absent-mindedly, her thoughts elsewhere. As she and Thea ascended the stairs to their chambers, she said in distress, "Oh dear, another matter of which I did not think to warn you. Pray do not mention your interest in growing fruits and vegetables, Thea. Flowers are unexceptionable, or even herbs, but people will think you odd if you talk of pears, potatoes, and parsnips."

Potatoes, parsnips, pregnancy, and prizefights, Thea thought rebelliously. How much easier her introduction to the ton would be if all she need do was avoid every word beginning with *P*.

"THEA?" A small, frightened voice woke her next morning. Sleepily she rolled over towards the centre of the bed. Penny was sitting up, her face a ghastly colour, shivering and clutching her stomach and her throat. "I think I'm about to be sick."

Throwing back the covers, Thea sprang out of bed and rushed to fetch the white china basin from the washstand. She tucked Penny's wrap about her shoulders, then donned her own, an aged, shapeless, blue flannel garment.

"I'll call Mama at once. She will know what to do."

"I'm going to die," Penny moaned.

Her long braids flapping against her back, Thea dashed across the passage to knock on the door. Meg opened it. She was already dressed, her cheeks pink, her dark eyes restored to their usual brightness.

"Thea, it is sunny out and there is a garden behind the inn. I'm going to walk for a while before breakfast. Will you and Penny..." She saw her sister's face as Thea stepped into the room. "Oh, what is wrong?"

"Penny is feeling dreadfully ill." With relief, she saw that her mother, too, was up, though not yet dressed. "Mama, pray come quickly."

As they all hurried to the other chamber, Lord Hazlewood approached from the far end of the passage. Not wanting to be rude, Thea stopped.

"Good morning, sir."

"Good morning, Miss Kilmore." He seemed larger than she remembered him, a solid, reliable figure in his dark blue coat, buckskin breeches, and top-boots. "Is something amiss?"

"Penny—Lady Kilmore—my sister-in-law is horridly queasy this morning. I am afraid something may be seriously wrong."

"I doubt it." His calm soothed her. "Nausea is not uncommon in Lady Kilmore's condition. Every one of my sisters has suffered the same distressing symptoms, without ever a serious problem. I daresay your mama will tell you there is no cause for alarm."

"Do you think so? Mama will know, of course, for she takes care of our tenants and neighbours when they are ill. Megan often goes with her, but I can never think what to say to them," she confided.

"Visiting invalids can be an ordeal." He smiled down at her, and she suddenly recalled that she was dressed only in her nightgown and wrap, her feet bare on the polished boards.

"I must go," she blurted out, and fled into the chamber.

Her mother turned from the bedside. "It is only morning sickness," she said.

"Only!" Penny wailed, huddled in misery over the basin.

"You will feel better presently, my dear. Meg, open the window, if you please. Fresh air will help, as will peace and quiet. Thea, pray get dressed. Go down with Meg and order weak tea and dry toast to be sent up for Penny."

As Thea dressed, the sound of voices floated up from the courtyard below the window. She thought she recognized Lord Hazlewood's and could not decide whether she hoped he was departing or not. Every time she saw him, she made a cake of herself, yet he set her at ease in a way she had rarely experienced.

She was pinning up her hair when Meg answered a knock on the door and found a waiter there with a tray.

"Lord Hazlewood's compliments, miss. Tea an' toast for Lady Kilmore."

Meg took the tray with an exclamation. "How did he know?"

"I told him Penny is unwell," said Thea guiltily. "He has several sisters, so morning sickness is no mystery to him. Come, Meg, I am ready. Let us go out to the garden for a few minutes.''

She pulled her sister out the door before her mother had a chance to bemoan her latest misdeed.

"Yet again, your marquis gallops to the rescue," Meg murmured. "A modern knight in shining armour, providing tea and toast instead of the heads of dragons and ogres."

"More practical, and *much* more agreeable," Thea pointed out.

Despite the season, the walled garden behind the inn was pleasant in the morning sun. Meg rhapsodized over autumn crocuses and spicy-scented chrysanthemums. A bed of Michaelmas daisies reminded Thea of Mr. DeVine's waistcoat and, discovering that Meg had been in no state last night to notice it, she described his resplendent attire.

"He claimed to be a pink of the ton," she said, "but Lord Hazlewood called him a Bond Street beau and a coxcomb."

Meg giggled. "Is not a coxcomb a vain braggart? What precisely do the other epithets signify?"

"I don't know, and I did not like to ask."

"I daresay he is bang up to the nines," said Meg, startling her sister with language she must have learned from Jason and upon which Mama would undoubtedly frown.

At that moment a window opened near where they were strolling and the Bond Street beau himself leaned out. "Miss Kilmore, shall you join us for breakfast?" he called.

While Thea hesitated, Meg responded gaily, "Certainly, sir, at once," and tugged her towards the nearest door.

"I suspect we ought not," Thea objected in a low voice. "Mama did not actually accept the invitation, and she is not here to chaperon us."

"You are sufficient chaperon for me, and I have had quite enough of my chamber."

The coffee-room was a still less desirable alternative, Thea had to admit, and she was old enough to chaperon her sister. They joined the gentlemen in their parlour.

Curtsying, Megan openly studied Mr. DeVine. Today he was more soberly clad, in buckskins, glossy gold-tasselled Hessians, and a bottle-green coat. Even his waistcoat was comparatively modest, grass green with a narrow gold stripe.

"I have been woefully taken in," Meg announced with a blithe unconcern for decorum. "Thea told me you are a pink of the ton, sir, but I do not consider your attire at all out of the common way."

Thea gasped in dismay, but both the gentlemen laughed.

"Now that is where you are wrong, Miss Megan," Mr. DeVine assured her. He went on to explain the importance of the cut of a coat, the tasteful choice of colours, the tying of a cravat, champagne in the boot-blacking . . .

Lord Hazlewood interrupted. "Not to mention the importance of not frightening the horses. Hence, Will's comparatively mundane dress by daylight." He turned to Thea. "Miss Kilmore, what may I order for your breakfast?"

When they were all seated and served, Meg, with a saucy smile, asked Mr. DeVine to explain the difference between a Bond Street beau and a pink of the ton.

"A Bond Street beau, ma'am, is a fribble with nothing on his mind but drawing all eyes to his appearance. To this end he will employ padded shoulders, false calves, pinched-in waist, a quantity of fobs, shirt points so high he cannot turn his head, and other vulgar excesses. A pink, on the other hand, while a leader of fashion and always precise to a pin, is also a sportsman and a man of easy manners, good address, and superior understanding."

"Bravo, coz! You could not praise yourself more highly."

Mr. DeVine shook his head in mock reproach. "My cousin Roderick favours the Corinthian set," he told the ladies mournfully.

"What is that?" Meg enquired.

"A sportsman, Miss Megan," said the marquis. "A man of easy manners, good address, and superior understanding, but with no more interest in his attire than to be neatly and properly clad. However, I don't aspire to belong to any set."

"Rod is a nonpareil. There is none other like him, especially in size! Miss Megan, allow me to recommend a slice of this delicious ham."

Lord Hazlewood asked Thea if her mother had agreed with his diagnosis of Penny's indisposition and went on to talk of his nieces and nephews. He had a dozen or more, aged from two to twenty. She tried to guess how old he was—four or five and thirty, she thought. Though by no means ill-favoured, he was not handsome in a conventional way; rather, his good-natured, tranquil cast of countenance made him attractive.

Nor was Mr. DeVine particularly handsome. His attraction was a lively, animated charm to which Megan's own vivacious spirit responded, to judge by the laughter Thea heard. Gradually the laughter grew less, and, glancing at her sister, she saw her biting her lip.

"Meg, dear, what is troubling you?"

She tried to smile. "I am stupidly anticipating today's journey. We . . . we have a long distance to travel, do we not?"

"Surely you do not intend to try to reach London today?" protested Mr. DeVine. "I doubt *we* shall make it in Rod's curricle, and he is a famous whip."

"Our brother is expecting us," said Thea doubtfully.

"If I might make a suggestion," Lord Hazlewood said, "I should be happy to reserve rooms for you at an inn in Biggleswade, halfway to Town, and to notify your brother of the delay."

"Oh, sir, what a splendid notion," cried Meg, her glow restored. "Thea, Mama will not object, will she?"

"I doubt it, but we had best go and ask her. We shall not delay you, Lord Hazlewood. I shall let you know directly."

As Mr. DeVine bowed over Meg's hand, he begged permission to call on her in Town.

"We shall be delighted to receive you, sir," she assured him. "We are to reside in Russell Square." She turned to take leave of the marquis.

Catching the look of utter consternation that crossed Will DeVine's face, Thea flinched. Though she knew Penny's house in Russell Square was far from the fashionable part of London, she had not realized the full significance of that fact.

Lord Hazlewood took her hand and smiled down at her. "May I presume to be included in Will's welcome?" he asked courteously.

"Of course, sir," she said, but she doubted either one would ever come to call.

CHAPTER THREE

"I CANNOT SEE why Lord Hazlewood called Mr. De-Vine a coxcomb," Meg said with some indignation as Thea closed the parlour door behind them. "I found him charming and elegant."

"I am sure the marquis was teasing his cousin."

"I'm glad they mean to call on us."

"Meg, pray do not count on it," Thea said anxiously. "You must not be disappointed if, as I fear, they were only being polite."

Meg laughed as she led the way up the stairs. "What care I? To be sure, I like Mr. DeVine very well, but what is one when I expect to meet dozens of eligible gentlemen? I daresay he will visit, though. Why should he not?"

"Because we shall be living somewhat out of the way of the quarters frequented by Society."

"Jason said Russell Square is no more than a mile from Mayfair and St. James's. Mr. DeVine claims to be a sportsman. He can hardly regard a mile as an insuperable distance!"

Not wanting to dampen Meg's spirits, which would fail soon enough once they were on the road, Thea did not contradict her. She suspected the distance was more in the mind than on the ground, the gulf between the haunts of the Upper Ten Thousand and the respectable residences of the wealthy bourgeoisie. Penny's father had been a lawyer. Though she was now a baroness, the ton would not welcome her with open arms nor flock to her house in the wrong part of Town.

Meg must have a proper Season, yet Thea could not let Penny be hurt. She had come to love the generous, forthright young woman her brother had unexpectedly taken to wife, and besides, without her house and fortune there would be no Season. If only she knew Jason better! Had he considered the difficulties and found solutions?

"Don't look so blue-devilled," Meg said, squeezing her arm. "Your marquis will call on us and we shall all have a wonderful time in London."

From the top of the stairs, a lean, red-nosed man watched their ascent with bleary, red-rimmed eyes. He was untidily dressed, with none-too-clean linen and a neckerchief in place of a cravat, yet he wore a heavy gold signet on one hand. As Meg stepped up to the landing, he reached out and chucked her under the chin.

"Hey, my pretty, what a devilish shame we didn't meet last night!" He leered at Meg, who stared at him in speechless astonishment. "Still, it's early yet. We've time for a quick tumble before—"

"Leave my sister alone!" said Thea in an icy voice she did not recognize as her own.

"Come on, Ilminster." The man who appeared behind him sounded impatient and disgusted. "I'll be damned if you're not still foxed. Leave the ladybirds be or we'll never get out of here."

"What, don't you fancy the hoity-toity beanpole? I've a mind to take this pretty little bit o' game with me to warm my bed tonight."

"Unhand me, sirrah!" Meg regained her wits. "I am no doxy."

Thea had no wish to bandy words with an inebriated boor; she gave her sister a push. Meg jerked away from the man's feeble grasp and took Thea's hand. As they fled, the second man said, "Those were no lightskirts, you sapskull. Can't you tell a lady when you hear one speak?"

"Damned if I ever chose a bit of muslin for her conversation," said the other sulkily.

Meg giggled. Breathless, they reached their chambers. Rather than alarm their mother and Penny by bursting in upon them, Thea thrust her sister into the opposite room. She closed the door behind them and leaned against it.

"'Unhand me, sirrah,' indeed. I daresay that came from one of your lending-library romances?"

"Yes, and it worked splendidly, did it not?"

Thea laughed. "Only because you spoke in accents of unmistakable gentility. No doubt those were two of the sporting gentlemen the innkeeper mentioned, who came to the boxing match."

"Sporting gentlemen—that's odd, is it not? What do you suppose the difference is between a gentlemanly sportsman, such as Mr. DeVine, and a sporting gentleman, such as that Ilminster? I should not describe him as a gentleman!"

"Not in his behaviour, certainly, but he may be a gentleman by rank. He wore a signet ring, and though his language was execrable, his accent was as refined as yours." And in tones of perfect refinement he had dubbed her a beanpole, she recalled with an internal grimace. She had always felt too tall beside her petite mother and sister, but it still hurt to hear it from a stranger's lips.

"Ilminster might be a title rather than a surname," Meg said in agreement. "But lord or no, his conduct makes Mr. DeVine's and Lord Hazlewood's appear positively saintly!"

"Gallant, certainly."

"Saintly. I asked Mr. DeVine where they spent the night. He said the landlord gave them two palliasses in a garret and the marquis's feet stuck out and rats nibbled his toes."

"He was roasting you." Thea shook her head, smiling. "Lord Hazlewood told me they had the chamber of an acquaintance they encountered in the coffee-room, who agreed to share with his friend. Meg, pray don't tell Mama about the ill-mannered Ilminster. It can only distress her."

"I shan't."

"Then let us go and persuade her to stop at Biggleswade. Oh dear, I promised not to keep the marquis waiting."

RODERICK CHARLES EDWARD DeVine, Marquis of Hazlewood, was quite content with a cup of excellent coffee and the *Times,* which he had set aside when the Misses Kilmore joined them. At the same time, he was deriving considerable amusement from his companion's disconsolate face. Crumbling a muffin in restless fingers, Will scowled at the window whence he had earlier called to the young ladies in the garden.

"Cat got your tongue?"

"What? Oh, go to the devil, Rod. It's just..." He was interrupted by the arrival of a maidservant with a folded sheet of paper addressed to Lord Hazlewood.

Rod opened it and found another inside, directed to Jason, Baron Kilmore, which he tossed on the table.

"The ladies wish to stay in Biggleswade tonight," he said, scanning the note. "We'd best be off if I'm to inform Kilmore of his family's whereabouts before he begins to wonder what has become of them."

Will picked up the second note. "I thought so," he said gloomily, reading the superscription.

"You can tell me what you thought, and why it should cast you into the dismals, once we are on the road."

While his groom saw to the harnessing of a team, he and Will donned their greatcoats, top hats and gloves. The half-dozen capes on Will's driving coat considerably reduced the difference in width, if not height, between them, since Rod himself, in defiance of fashion, had but one.

Paying the reckoning, they took their leave of Percival and went out to the courtyard.

"We shall drive straight through to Town in the curricle," Rod told his young groom. "With Mr. DeVine's man to share the driving, you should have no difficulty managing it with the carriage, but if you have any trouble, put up somewhere on the way and come on tomorrow."

"No, dash it, Rod." Will protested. "Would you deprive me of my valet overnight?"

"I should not dare. You may join him in the carriage."

Climbing into the lighter vehicle, Will laughed and shook his head. "Not I. I shall just have to keep to my room until Purvis arrives. Let's go, coz."

The two-wheeled vehicle, with its resilient C-springs, rolled smoothly out of The Haycock's courtyard and turned south on the busy Great North Road. The sunny day, with an autumnal crispness in the air, was perfect for driving. Frost had touched willows and poplars with yellow. In some of the flat fields along the way, farmhands harvested turnips and onions. In others, sturdy, patient Suffolk punches drew ploughs through the rich soil, the long, straight furrows lengthening behind them.

The four horses harnessed to the curricle were less patient. The groom, with his master's title and wealth to back him, had selected The Haycock's most mettlesome cattle. For the first mile Rod had to concentrate on handling the ribbons, until the team settled down to working together and he could turn his attention to his cousin.

Will had lost his disgruntled expression. Now cheerfully insouciant, he was softly whistling "Cherry Ripe." He noticed Rod's ironic glance and said, "A pity about the Kilmores."

"A pity?"

"Miss Megan's a pretty chit, and lively, though it's no good pretending she's up to snuff, any more than her sister is. Still, with a little Town bronze and a new wardrobe, she'd be a pocket Venus, I suspect. I wouldn't have minded pursuing the acquaintance, but it won't do. I was afraid they must be connections of Jason Kilmore. His sisters, no less! The fellow's a wastrel, a regular loose fish."

"I'd hardly put it so strongly. A trifle ramshackle, but received everywhere. It was his father, not he, who ruined the family by deep play. Jason was never guilty, so far as I know, of any worse than living a fashionable life beyond his means."

"And his indiscreet amours! Even though he was received by the ton, mamas warned off their daughters. The man's a gazetted fortune-hunter."

"To seek to mend the family fortunes through marriage is not an uncommon nor a dishonourable goal," said Rod tolerantly.

"Not by abduction. It's said he tried to carry off the Larkin heiress, the one who married Trevelyan. And now he's persuaded some Cit's daughter to the altar, or more likely to the anvil at Gretna Green."

"What makes you think Lady Kilmore is not of gentle birth?" Rod asked, though he had long since come to the same conclusion.

"A house in Bloomsbury. Damme, it's plain as the nose on your face. Kilmore has wed a Cit's daughter for her money, and Society is going to change its tune."

"You are probably right," Rod admitted with regret.

"There you are, then. One can't go paying calls in Russell Square."

"My dear William, *you* may not. I trust *my* consequence is sufficient to survive a visit to even so plebeian an address."

"You mean to call?"

"I do. Miss Kilmore is a true original, and they are few and far between. Shy as bedamned, yet throwing discretion to the winds, with no regard for conventional propriety, when her family's comfort is threatened! I don't know when I have been as well entertained."

"Miss Kilmore?" Will was astonished. "I thought her dull and gauche. But then, you seem to find everything amusing. For all you look as if butter wouldn't melt in your mouth, I sometimes wonder if you give a tinker's curse for convention and propriety. Which is deuced odd, when my aunt is so devilish high in the instep."

Rod considered this for a moment. "Say rather that I have a different notion of propriety from Mother's, and will not let myself be bound by convention. To refuse an acquaintanceship that promises pleasure merely because Society may frown appears to me to be sheer perversity."

"Gammon! Philosophize if you will, but admit that it is simply another of your chivalrous impulses. You don't wish the Misses Kilmore to suffer for their brother's misdeeds. I'd give a monkey to see you bring them into fashion."

"I have no such ambitious plan, I assure you," he said with a lazy smile. "Now hush while I pass these sheep or we shall come to grief."

Directed by a drover, three tan-and-white sheepdogs kept the flock bound for Smithfield Market to one side of the road. Rod drove past at a slow trot, alert for stragglers. The horses were uneasy. When a fat, bleating ewe darted right in front of them, they shied and tried to bolt. With the quick reactions and strong yet sensitive hands of an expert driver, Rod held them, and a dog instantly turned the sheep back.

"I don't know which is more admirable," said Will with a grin as they passed the front of the flock and returned to their own side of the road, "your skill or the dogs'."

"Oh, the dogs', every time. I control four harnessed horses, which are moderately intelligent animals. They control several dozen unrestrained sheep, quite the silliest animals I know."

Laughing, Will agreed. They went on to talk of horses and dogs, abandoning, by tacit consent, the subject of the Misses Kilmore's future.

CHAPTER FOUR

THE TRIM, ELEGANT FIGURE of Jason, Baron Kilmore, was as out of place in the bare entrance hall as a butterfly in a midwinter garden. There was no carpet, nor pictures on the bare walls, the only furnishings being a pair of dingy deal chairs that appeared to have escaped from the kitchens.

Jason's darkly handsome face wore an expression of shock. "Penny, you look as if you have one foot in the grave!"

Thea frowned at her brother. That was hardly a tactful way to greet the bride he had not seen for a month—which was not to say it was untrue. Stretching the last part of the journey over two days had helped Meg but drained the last of Penny's energy. She sank onto a chair, hid her pallid face in her hands, and burst into tears.

"I'm increasing," she wailed.

"Increasing?" he said blankly. "Oh, is that what makes you look so ill? You had best lie down at once. Come, let me take you up to your chamber, my dear." He helped her to stand, then, his arm about her waist, turned to the others with a distracted air. "I haven't hired abigails, as I thought you would wish to choose your own."

"Thea." Penny reached out to her with a sob.

"I shall come with you." Thea moved to Penny's side and Jason released her.

"Mama, Meg, are you more in need of rest or refreshment?" He ran his hand through his hair. "Dash it, I'm not used to playing hostess. Oh, there you are, Mrs. Creswell. Mama, the housekeeper. Give her what orders you will. I must go with Penny."

Thea, supporting Penny towards the stairs, glanced back and saw a stout woman in black curtsying to her mother.

"So you have hired *some* servants?" she said with unwonted asperity to Jason as he joined them.

"Yes, of course, but they are less than satisfactory, I fear. I have no experience at selecting any but valets and grooms."

"And you have bought some furniture?" The stairs, like the hall, were bare of carpet.

"Beds, a table for the morning-room, the absolute necessities. I have not had time. You wouldn't believe what a mess Vaughn left the place in, after removing everything of value. Besides, I thought Penny would enjoy choosing furnishings. Penny, had I known you were ill, I never would have expected you to come to Town."

"But I wanted to come," Penny wept, plodding up the stairs. Having begun to cry, she was too tired to stop.

Jason made a move as if to take her in his arms, but at that moment a white-aproned maid appeared at the top of the stairs.

"Will I bring 'ot water, m'lord?"

"Hot water, hot bricks, warming pan. My lady is unwell."

"And tea, if you please," Thea added as Jason thrust his handkerchief into his wife's hand, provoking a new outburst of tears. "Hush, Penny dear. You will feel better as soon as you lie down."

Murmuring words of comfort, Thea led Penny after Jason, to a dressing-room as large as her own chamber at home. The walls were painted palest green, and the curtains at the window were a darker green sprigged with buttercup yellow, matching the Wilton carpet and the upholstery of a comfortable chaise longue. A well-polished wardrobe, dressing-table, and chest of drawers gleamed in the late-afternoon sunshine slanting through the window. A full-length cheval glass reflected the cheerful flames of the fire that kept the October chill at bay.

Thea thought it charming. Penny clung to her, her face buried in the handkerchief, sniffling.

With a helpless, anxious glance, Jason said, "If you don't care for it you can change it, and anything in our bedchamber, of course." He gestured towards a door. Penny sobbed the harder.

Seating her on the chaise longue and untying her bonnet, Thea said apologetically, "She is exhausted."

"Penny, you need not fear that I'll disturb you. I shall sleep in my dressing-room."

Though Thea suspected that was quite the wrong thing to say, she did not feel capable of mediating between husband and wife. She was a spinster, and likely to remain one, and besides, she scarcely knew her brother. "I shall help her to bed now," she told him.

"My dear, I'll come and see you later." He patted Penny's shoulder awkwardly and left.

Penny sank back on the chaise longue and gazed at Thea with despair in her eyes. "He is not at all glad that I am with child."

"I doubt that he has properly grasped the fact that he is to be a father," Thea soothed her. "He was too distressed by your fatigue."

"I must look a fright. No wonder he was vexed that I came to London."

"Not vexed! Concerned for your health, my dear."

"He too called me 'my dear,' not 'my love' as he was used to." Biting her lip, Penny failed to suppress a sob. "I know he is tired of me. He only married me for my fortune, because Henrietta changed her mind. Did you know he tried and failed to abduct another well-dowered young lady once? He told me her name—Alison."

"No, I did not know," said Thea, shocked. Then she pointed out in her brother's defence, "But he did not abduct Henrietta. That elopement was her notion and arranged by Jason and her father to please her. What a silly goose she was!"

"I daresay that's why he liked me better, only now I am being just as goosish." She dissolved in tears again. "Indeed, I cannot help it."

Thea was about to promise Penny she would feel better after a good night's sleep when she remembered the morning sickness. Nor was she able wholeheartedly to affirm that Jason had neither married Penny for her money nor tired of her since. His record was against him.

Ten years ago, when Jason finished his schooling, he had joined their father in a life of dissipation in London. Following the late baron's example, he had rarely visited his home in Northumberland. He became a stranger to his mother and sisters. The discovery that he had inherited little but a pile of debts only led him to seek a wealthy bride so as to continue as before.

Then, late last spring, he had arrived unexpectedly at Newkirk when the hillsides were yellow with fragrant gorse and long-tailed lambs skipped in the fields. Thea wondered now whether he had come to avoid recriminations after his failed abduction of the unknown Alison.

Whatever the reason for his visit, for the first time since long-ago school holidays he took an interest in his estate—what was left of it after their father had sold off most of the farms. He looked at his dilapidated home, his shabby mother and sisters, and he did not like what he saw. When next he came north he was accompanied by his betrothed, Henrietta White, a rich young lady whose Cit father was willing to purchase a title for her by providing the wherewithal to restore Newkirk to its former prosperity. With them were Penelope Bryant and Dr. Angus Knox, another ill-matched couple on their way to Gretna.

But Henrietta had despised the ancient, weathered manor, and insulted his threadbare family. Instead, Jason had married Penny, whom he had met on the road north to Gretna. Whether he had taken her to wife because he loved her, to save her from her uncle's persecution, or simply for her fortune, Thea could not guess.

"I am sure he will be glad you are *enceinte* once the news has sunk in," she said with as much conviction as she could muster. "And Mama says the first two months of pregnancy are often the most difficult."

The maid, clucking sympathetically, brought hot water and returned, once Penny was tucked up in her warm bed, with a tray of tea and soup. After drinking a little of each, Penny fell asleep. She did not stir when, a few minutes later, the dowager came in briefly to see how she was.

As Thea left to go and find her own chamber to change for dinner, Jason returned. Before she closed the door behind her, she saw him standing by the bed, gazing down at his sleeping wife, but she could not see his expression.

Besides her trunk, Thea's chamber contained nothing but a bed, bare of hangings, and a deal kitchen chair like those in the entrance hall below. The window, overlooking Russell Square, was swathed in cheap brown holland. Despite the sea-coal fire glowing in the grate, the uncarpeted floor made the room feel chilly. She noticed that several of the floorboards appeared to have been recently replaced.

Meg's room, next door, was exactly the same, she discovered when she went to help her sister button her pink muslin gown.

"You have recovered quickly," she said, unpacking a shawl and draping it about Meg's shoulders.

"Yes, stopping every few miles for a walk made all the difference. I'm only sorry it did not help Penny. I do think Jason might have made more effort to furnish her house before we arrived!"

"He took great pains to make her dressing-room and bedchamber pleasant. I cannot believe he does not love her."

"Of course he loves her. Why should he marry her, else?"

Though Thea did not disillusion her romantic sister, she could not help recalling that Jason had been equally ready to marry Henrietta or Alison. At best that indicated a shocking fickleness in his affections.

They went down together, joining their mother and brother in the morning-room, since drawing-room and dining-room were both unfurnished. An aged, tottery butler appeared to serve dinner. Thea held her breath as he carried in the plain white china dishes one by one, in imminent danger of dropping each. Jason dismissed him as soon as everything was on the table.

"I interviewed him one morning, and he is comparatively sprightly before noon," he explained with a wry smile.

The meal was as simple as the country fare the Kilmores were used to at Newkirk, but half the food was burnt and the rest underdone.

Jason hacked at a charred piecrust as tough as shoe leather. "My apologies," he said. "Mama, since Penny is out of sorts, I hope you will take charge of the household. Dismiss what servants you will and hire others."

"Oh dear, I have no notion how to go about it in London," said the dowager anxiously. "At home one has one's own people."

"Penny ran her father's household," Thea reminded her. "She will know what to do."

"I don't want her troubled," Jason insisted.

"We shall have to consult her about furnishings. She will want to choose colours and patterns."

"I can have tradesmen bring samples to the house for her to examine at leisure. Nonetheless, I wish I had had time to do more. The repairs were only completed the day before I expected you to arrive."

"Repairs?" asked Meg. "I noticed the new floorboards in my chamber."

"Penny's uncle was not satisfied with removing everything of value," said Jason grimly. "He took his revenge for the loss of her fortune with an axe. Holes in floors and walls, the stair rails smashed to pieces, broken glass everywhere." He ran his fingers through his dark hair in remembered frustration. "For pity's sake, don't tell her how bad it was."

"It sounds horrid," Meg admitted. "But we cannot live in empty rooms for long just because Penny is not well. Suppose Mr. DeVine and Thea's marquis come to call!"

"Thea's marquis?" he said, startled. "You mean Hazlewood? It was obliging in him to send his boy with your note, but I thought him no more than a chance-met acquaintance. Has he been particular in his attentions, then, Thea?"

"Oh no!" she cried in confusion. "You misunderstand Meg's silly way of referring to him. He was most agreeable and all that is chivalrous, but his concern was for Meg's and Penny's indispositions, not for me."

"You mean he . . ."

At that moment, Meg attempted to spear a potato with her fork. Hard and slippery as soap, it shot across the table, knocking over a gravy-boat and ricocheting to land in Lady Kilmore's lap. His question forgotten, Jason jumped up to avoid the flood of watery gravy.

Meg collapsed in giggles. "It's just as well there is no carpet," she gasped.

"The cook must go," pronounced her mother resolutely, dabbing at her skirts with a napkin.

Thea breathed a sigh of relief. Had Jason pressed her, she might have been forced to confess that, far from wishing to fix his interest with her, Lord Hazlewood doubtless considered her an ill-bred hoyden.

She sighed again, with regret. If only she dared hope for another chance to gain his good opinion.

LORD HAZLEWOOD ALLOWED the Kilmore ladies three
days to recover from their journey and settle in Town.
Then, his olive-green-and-silver-liveried tiger up behind, he drove his curricle towards Bloomsbury.

"Cor blimey, guv, where're we going?" the boy demanded as they left Oxford Street behind them. "Di'n't
you say we was jus' paying a morning call?"

"In Russell Square."

"There ain't no nobs living in Russell bloody Square
'cepting Lord Kilmore, as I took that letter to, and from
what I've 'eard 'e ain't zackly top-o'-the-trees. Wotcher
want to get mixed up wiv 'im for?"

Passing the British Museum and turning up Mon-
tague Street, Rod asked himself the same question. His
family, following Will's lead, would undoubtedly dub
the visit one of his quixotic whims. They'd not be altogether wrong.

While he doubted the Misses Kilmore would be deliberately ostracized, despite the baron's misdeeds and
their unfashionable address, they might find it difficult
to enter the highest circles. Kilmore was at best a care-
for-nobody, and the dowager, by what he had seen of
her, was of a retiring disposition. Neither was likely to
make a push to obtain invitations. His brief encounter
with the new Lady Kilmore suggested that she was not
the sort of vulgar upstart who attempted to thrust her
way into Society. If she did, she'd only succeed in setting up people's backs.

The young ladies did not deserve to suffer through no
fault of their own. To that extent he admitted to chivalrous motives; yet there was more.

Miss Kilmore's unconventional behaviour did not
merely entertain him, it intrigued him. He admired the
way she overcame her natural timidity when her fami-

ly's well-being was at stake. Brought up in the remote wilds of the country, she was as naïve as her sister, but with a hint of unworldliness quite unlike Miss Megan's frank enjoyment of Will's flirting.

What went on behind that quiet, thoughtful face? She interested him more than any woman he had met in his years on the Town: the hopeful debutantes with ambitious mamas; widows amorous or impecunious who set their caps at him; high-flying Cyprians in search of a wealthy protector.

Finding something lacking in one and all, Rod had courteously avoided every snare. Perhaps, if he succeeded in penetrating her reserve, he would find that Miss Kilmore, too, had nothing to offer him. But he suspected—he hoped—that she was different.

"'Ere we are, guv."

Lord Hazlewood reined in his greys in front of a large house on the west side of Russell Square, one of a fine modern terrace. In the garden in the centre of the square, trees displayed their autumn russet and gold above flower-beds as well kept as any in Mayfair. Battling the stiff, chilly breeze, an old man was raking leaves into neat heaps.

It seemed a prosperous neighbourhood. Then Rod looked up at the stone-and-brick façade of the Kilmores' house and was puzzled to see row upon row of windows untidily draped in cheap brown holland.

He took a calling-card from its case and passed it to his tiger. "Ask if the ladies are receiving visitors," he instructed.

"Ho—ladies, is it?"

As Billy hopped down and dashed across the pavement to ring the doorbell, his master noticed that the boy's wrists and ankles protruded from his livery again.

He was growing too big for his present employment.
Time to give the lad a choice of becoming stable-boy
and working with the horses he loved, or under-
footman, wearing a new suit of the smart uniform he
was so proud of. If he chose the latter, he'd have to learn
to curb his impudent tongue!

A maid trimly clad in black with a white apron and
cap answered the door. Billy spoke to her, then returned to the curricle to announce, "She says 'is lordship's out but the ladies is at 'ome, if your lordship
don't mind waiting a minute or two."

Rod stepped down and handed over the reins, with
orders to walk the horses. Entering the house, he looked
around with interest. The hall was of elegant propor-
tions, with a fine staircase, but furnished only with a
couple of deal chairs, on one of which the maid set his
hat and gloves. The other was already encumbered by
a glossy, curly-brimmed beaver, a pair of York tan
gloves, and a silver-topped cane he thought he recognized.

CHAPTER FIVE

ROD'S AMUSED SURMISE proved correct. When the Kilmores' maid ushered him into a small room at the front of the house, the dapper figure standing at the window overlooking the square swung round.

"Oh, it's you, coz," said Will sheepishly.

"Not one of your more brilliant observations. I did say I meant to call, you may remember."

Will dodged the reminder that he had vowed Russell Square to be beyond the pale. "I say, devilish smoky, ain't it?" He gestured at the shabby table and chairs. "Why not show us into the drawing-room?"

"Perhaps it is not prepared for visitors, as they did not expect any," Rod suggested, his tone dry.

Abashed, Will smoothed the sleeve of his mulberry coat. "Only proper to ask after the invalids," he muttered. Raising his voice, he added, "Besides, they won't have any other callers here at the back of beyond, so I felt it my duty to come and cheer them up."

His face bid fair to match his coat as Miss Megan appeared in the doorway. Her hair cut short in a froth of curls, she was fresh and pretty in a simple but modish gown of white muslin sprigged with rosebuds, a pink silk shawl about her shoulders. With a reproachful glance at Will, and very much on her dignity, she advanced into the room to curtsy to the marquis.

"How delightful to see you again, my lord."

"The pleasure is mine, ma'am. I trust you are quite restored to health?"

"Oh yes, I recovered quickly, thanks to your suggestion of dividing the rest of the journey in two. It was prodigious amiable in you to go to the trouble of reserving rooms for us at Biggleswade." She favoured him with an enchanting smile. Will looked glum as she turned to him and said coolly, "Good day, Mr. DeVine."

Her sister was hesitating on the threshold, the slender grace of her figure accentuated by a new gown of cerulean blue kerseymere. She had put off her cap, revealing the sheen of her smooth, dark hair. She seemed half poised to flee, so Rod went to meet her. At his approach, her gaze descended to his top waistcoat button. He did not suppose that she was admiring the circle of polished horn.

"Miss Kilmore, I am happy to see you safely arrived in Town."

"Thank you for calling, sir. It is most kind when we are situated in such an unfashionable location."

"No part of Town can be deemed unfashionable when such fair ladies dwell there." The compliment slipped from his lips with practised facility. He cursed himself as she coloured and her gaze fell to the next button down. Commonplace courtesies were not the way to set her at ease, but he knew what would. "May I enquire after Lady Kilmore's health?"

"My mother will be down shortly, sir."

"I shall be glad to renew the acquaintance, but I was actually referring to your sister-in-law," he teased gently.

"Oh, Penny, of course. How silly of me." She risked an upward peek. His expression must have reassured her, for her dark, apprehensive eyes met his and she went on, "Poor Penny suffers dreadfully every morning. She is quite well in the afternoons, though—fortunately. I do not know how we should go on without her."

"No?" he asked, curious.

"She has lived in London all her life. She knows where to find furniture-makers and servants and the best modistes, and how to deal with them. We have new gowns already, and abigails, and she replaced the cook Jason hired, who even managed to make eggs inedible. The new butler starts tomorrow, the housekeeper is on probation...but you cannot be interested in such petty domestic details."

"On the contrary, ma'am." He cast a quizzical glance about the room. "Lady Kilmore's taste in modistes is irreproachable, but I dare to question her choice of furniture-makers."

Like a candle in a Chinese paper lantern, her smile lit her face with a soft glow. "Is it not horrid? Penny is not to blame. Jason bought a few necessary pieces to last until she could refurnish her house."

"It must have been badly furnished indeed if it was worse than what you have now."

"Oh no, everything was of the best," she assured him earnestly. "Penny's father was very rich. You see, her uncle was excessively angry when she married Jason, because he lost control of her fortune. He stole everything in the house and then set about wrecking it. Jason has spent weeks in rendering it habitable."

Rod frowned. "Both greedy and vengeful. Has your brother called in a magistrate?"

"No. He says it would be difficult to prove, and Penny is afraid of Mr. Vaughn. Jason does not wish to distress her in her delicate condition."

"Understandable." He wondered why her attention had suddenly returned to his waistcoat buttons, her cheeks now scarlet.

"I beg your pardon, sir," she said in a low voice. "I vowed I would not mention that subject again. My wits have gone a-begging."

"Fustian!" he said roundly, sternly controlling his twitching lips. "You mean Lady Kilmore's condition, I collect? My dear Miss Kilmore, I hope you will always say to me exactly what you please, though observing discretion when others are about, to be sure. I promise never to be shocked."

To his surprised delight, her smile glimmered again. "Never?"

With a grin, he admitted, "Perhaps it would be safer to say hardly ever."

Megan, standing by the window with Will, called to her sister. "Thea, do you think Mama would let me go with Mr. DeVine to Kew Gardens to see the flowers?"

"I don't know. Is it not some distance out of London?"

"Only ten miles or so, Miss Kilmore," Will assured her.

"Not far enough to make you ill, Meg, but I expect Mama will insist that you have a chaperon."

"Naturally my invitation includes you, ma'am, if you care to go."

"Thea is more interested in growing fruits and vegetables than flowers," Meg revealed, laughing.

"Vegetables!" At Will's astonished exclamation, Thea flinched, her hard-won composure shattered.

Casting a minatory glance at his tactless cousin, Rod said with his usual calm, "I recall your knowledge of different kinds of pears, Miss Kilmore. Perhaps you would enjoy a visit to Covent Garden Market, to see the produce of the whole country and half the world."

"No, I say, Rod," Will protested. "Not at all the thing."

"The crowds are far from genteel," he conceded, watching Thea, "and one must go at daybreak for the widest variety, but I believe you would find it interesting."

Taking a deep breath, she looked him full in the face. "Thank you, Lord Hazlewood, I should like to go."

"If Mama permits," Meg reminded her.

"What am I asked to permit?" came a quiet voice, and the dowager entered the room, followed by her red-headed daughter-in-law, a Junoesque figure in green sarcenet.

After an exchange of greetings, Meg explained. "Lord Hazlewood has invited Thea to visit Covent Garden Market. At dawn! I would not go for the world!"

"Oh, Thea," said young Lady Kilmore regretfully, "I wish I could go to keep you company."

"So do I, Penny dear, but it is out of the question. Mama, I shall be perfectly safe with Lord Hazlewood, and surely I am past the age to need a chaperon."

The dowager dithered. Patently, she had no desire to brave the vulgar crowds at that hour, nor did she want to disappoint her daughter. She shrank from offending the marquis, but equally she did not care to entrust Thea alone to him, whatever her age.

With the last, Rod agreed. "Cannot your maid accompany you, Miss Kilmore?" he suggested.

This solution was greeted with relief, and Will took his turn to propose his outing to Kew. "Everyone accepted *my* invitation," he pointed out smugly to Rod as they departed a short time later.

"What possessed you to plan an excursion to Kew?"

"I discovered that Meg adores flowers."

"And what flowers, pray tell, do you expect to find at this time of year?"

"There's bound to be something blooming in the hothouses," said Will optimistically. "What the devil possessed *you* to invite Miss Kilmore to the market? Not at all a suitable place for a lady."

"Miss Kilmore is no ordinary lady," said Rod, unruffled.

"How ODD in the marquis to invite you to Covent Garden Market, Thea," said her mother, perplexed. "Are you quite sure you did not misunderstand a reference to the theatre?"

"No, Mama."

"One does not attend the theatre at daybreak," Penny pointed out.

"Then you must have been talking of parsnips. Oh dear, I did warn you not to."

"It was my fault," Meg confessed. "I'm sorry, Thea. Mr. DeVine was shocked, I'm afraid, but the marquis took it quite in his stride."

"I fear Lord Hazlewood appears to be a trifle eccentric." The dowager sounded vaguely worried.

Thea flared up. "He is all that is obliging!"

"Yes, my love, but I cannot help wondering why he is taking such pains for strangers with no conceivable claim to his benevolence."

"I heard Mr. DeVine mention 'another quixotic start,' " said Thea hesitantly.

"Oh, that is all right, then," her mother said with relief. "If it is a habit with him to help lame dogs over stiles, he doubtless simply regards us as a cause for charitable concern."

"I am not a lame dog!" said Meg, her face pink with indignation.

Penny laughed. "Not now, but the epithet fitted both you and me when we arrived at The Haycock."

"I suppose so. I wish Mr. DeVine had not seen me when I was so odiously ill and dressed in the dowdiest clothes." Her attention was caught by something outside the window. "Penny, look. Two drays just pulled up in the street. I believe it is the painters and paper-hangers."

With the competent assurance Thea admired, Penny took charge. At her bidding, workmen were soon busy throughout the house in an orderly chaos of buckets and paste pots, brushes and ladders.

The ladies escaped for a few hours to attend fittings at the dressmaker's. When they returned, laden with packages, the house reeked of paint. Already tired, Penny found the smell unbearable, and she was further distressed to find Jason not yet come home.

Begging Thea to go with her, she retired to the chaise longue in her dressing-room to rest before dinner.

"I have scarcely set eyes on him since we arrived," she said unhappily, having dismissed the new abigail the two of them shared. "He leaves before I am well enough to go down in the morning, and if he returns for dinner he goes out again afterwards. What do you think he is doing?"

"It must be something important to keep him from you," said Thea, seated on the stool at the dressing-table. "You must not trouble yourself about it."

"But why does he not tell me?"

"He has been used to his freedom these many years. I daresay it does not even dawn on him to account to anyone for his coming and going. You ought to ask him."

"I could not bear him to think me a nagging wife, especially when I fear he already regrets having married me." She clasped Thea's hand. "Will you ask him where he goes?"

"If you wish," she said, with deep misgivings.

"I wish I had let Angus stop at The Haycock, as he intended!" Penny cried. "I'd be his wife now, and Henrietta would be Jason's. The life of a doctor's wife might be dull, but even if he, too, had regretted marrying me, it would be less painful because I did not love him."

"What happened at Wansford?" Thea asked, long-suppressed curiosity getting the better of her.

"That was the first time I made a deliberate effort to meet Jason again, before Angus and I were taken up in his coach. He and Henrietta were ahead of us. He had mentioned that they meant to take luncheon in Stamford, and I persuaded Angus to go on there instead of stopping at The Haycock. Then Henrietta insisted on letting her dratted kitten play in the meadow by the river at Wansford. When Angus and I reached the bridge, I saw them. I made Angus stop the carriage and went to help Jason rescue a mole from the kitten." A reminiscent smile played on her lips, then faded. "I wish we had driven on!"

"Well I do not, for I'd never have known you. How dreadful it would have been to have Henrietta for a sister-in-law." All too clearly Thea recalled the spoiled girl's careless contempt.

There was a tapping on the door and Meg put her head around it. "Penny, you are not sleeping? Now that I have seen the colour of the walls, I want to consult you about the hangings for my chamber." She flitted in, her arms full of swatches of gauzy material. "It is going to look simply splendid."

Distracted from her woes, Penny cheered up. Thea left them comparing shades of rose-pink, Meg's favourite colour, and went to her own chamber.

Crossing the room to the window, she watched the lamplighter make his rounds of the square. She was troubled. Penny's megrims disturbed her, and she was vexed with Jason for the unexplained absences that only made matters worse. And now that she had leisure for reflection, she realized that her spirits were low on her own account.

Lord Hazlewood's unexpected visit, his invitation to the market, had raised hopes that she had found a friend who accepted her despite her shyness and her proclivity for committing *faux pas*. She should have known better. After all, she had heard Will DeVine speak as if his cousin's acts of benevolence were frequent enough to be a joke. To the marquis she was no more than—in Mama's phrase—a lame dog. The words had annoyed Meg, yet Thea could not resent his generosity.

Nor could she bring herself to reject the semblance of friendship. She believed him sincere when he told her she could say anything to him. When she was with him, she would dismiss the guard on her tongue.

Instead, she must set a guard on her heart. The Marquis of Hazlewood was a man with whom she'd find it all too easy to fall in love, but she must never forget that to him she was merely an object of charity.

She smiled ruefully at her reflection in the window. In King Arthur's day, knights in shining armour wed the damsels in distress they were called upon to rescue. In unromantic modern times, no wealthy, distinguished nobleman was likely to ask a penniless, maladroit spinster to be his bride.

Thea was glad to have her gloomy musing interrupted by her sister's arrival. "Have you chosen a colour for your chamber?" she asked.

"Yes, and it will look very well, but . . ." Meg's voice trailed to silence.

"But?"

"Did you hear what Mr. DeVine was saying just before we joined them in the morning-room?"

Thea shook her head. "You did, I collect."

"He only called because we will not have any other visitors and he felt it his duty to cheer us up. I wish Penny would sell this house and buy one in Mayfair."

"Meg, you never said so to her!"

"I thought I ought to ask you first."

"Then you have guessed that it is out of the question. For a start, because of the insult to her father's situation. Then the ingratitude, when she has been so good to us, not only allowing but pressing Jason to bring us to Town and buy us new clothes. And to suggest such a thing when her health is so uncertain!"

"I didn't suggest it, Thea, not to Penny. I can see that it's impossible. I will not mention it again, I promise." Meg sighed. "Things never turn out as you expect, do they? I suppose I should be glad that Mr. DeVine has a strong sense of duty."

"Cheer up, love. I don't believe for a moment that duty brought him to our unfashionable doorstep, and duty certainly will not take him to Kew Gardens. The lure is your pretty face."

"Well, I do think he admires me a little, but I cannot rely upon him to offer for me. If I am to find a husband, I must meet other gentlemen. What a pity Lord Hazlewood is so old, and so large! He is quite nice and I should like to be a marchioness, but he makes me feel like a beetle talking to a bull."

Thea laughed. "A butterfly, Meg. No one could ever mistake you for a beetle. Now go and put on your new wings. It is time to change for dinner."

"With all the wet paint about, I'll not risk my new gown. I shall suffer through one more evening in that horrid old pink rag."

As Meg pattered out, the new abigail came in. Thea found the gaunt, grey-haired woman somewhat intimidating, but she had excellent references and she reminded Penny of the dearly loved maid her uncle Vaughn had dismissed. Penny had never heard from Nancy, who had been her nurse. She still missed her and worried about her fate.

"Her ladyship says she'll dine in her room, miss," said Farden now, setting a ewer of hot water on the washstand. "You'll be wearing your new gown?"

"No, the old one, because of the wet paint," Thea said absently. "Farden, is Lady Kilmore feeling ill?"

"Just dog-tired, miss."

Worrying about Penny and Meg, Thea spoke scarcely a word while the woman helped her change and dressed her hair. She went down determined to tackle Jason on behalf of both, if he dined at home.

Her brother had sent a message to say he would be out until late.

DURING THE NIGHT, the fine weather broke. Thea woke to the sound of rain being dashed against her window by gusts of wind. In the square, sodden leaves lay in drifts and the few passers-by hugged their overcoats about them. Hoping that Jason would not leave the snug haven of the house, Thea went down to breakfast.

He was there already, preoccupied with a sheet of paper on which he made occasional notes as he ate. Greeting her, his handsome face sombre, he said, "Mama is with Penny, as usual. It's a cursed nuisance, this morning sickness."

"Yes, but she is better in the afternoons, as you would know if you were ever at home." She was not quite bold enough to ask outright where he went and on what business. "Surely you will not go out today?"

"I cannot let foul weather coop me up. Darlington is expecting me at noon, and I am engaged to meet a number of others at Brooks's later. Fortunately, I have a wide acquaintance among the ton."

Fortunately! How was she to tell Penny that her husband spent his days amusing himself with his friends? She made no effort to keep a certain dryness from her tone as she enquired, "May we hope to receive invitations from some of your acquaintance? Meg is eager to enter the social whirl."

"I have mentioned that you are all in Town, of course, but it's the ladies who issue invitations. Mama must take you to call on *her* acquaintances." His mind elsewhere, he scribbled some figures on the paper near his plate.

Thea tried in vain to picture her vague, retiring mama calling uninvited on Society hostesses, with three young ladies in tow. She was not at all sure the dowager even had any acquaintance in London. Since her marriage she had resided in Northumberland, never setting foot farther south than Kendal.

Had they all escaped from their isolation for nothing? Meg *must* have the chance to make a respectable match. Mr. DeVine and Lord Hazlewood were their only hope.

CHAPTER SIX

"IT'S STOPPED RAINING, my lord, and it's a bit warmer, though it's still overcast."

Rod blinked up at his valet's stolid, candlelit face. "What the...?"

"Covent Garden, my lord," said Pelham with deep disapproval. "You did ask me to wake you before dawn the first morning it didn't look like rain."

"Oh yes, quite right." He sat up, the draught from his movement making the candle flame flicker. "What time is it? Send Billy to Russell Square with the note I gave you the other day. Did you order the carriage?"

Hurriedly dressing, he felt an unexpected tingle of anticipation, the excitement of a schoolboy rising early to raid an unsuspecting farmer's apple orchard. A mere association of ideas, no doubt—leaving his comfortable bed at daybreak to visit the fruit market. What the devil had possessed him to suggest anything so harebrained?

The plain fact of the matter was that he had been unable to stand by without trying to extricate Thea from her painful embarrassment. He had said the first thing that came into his head and she, full of pluck, had accepted his invitation despite Will's remonstrances.

Will was right, of course, that the market was no place for a lady. Gentlemen might stroll through on occasion after a long night on the Town, the sort he had not indulged in since he'd taken Sue under his protection. Though she was his mistress and the widow of an actor, in her way Sue was as conventional as his mother; she'd be shocked to hear of his latest freak.

He wondered whether the reality of the market would shock Thea. Her sheltered upbringing could have given her no notion of the vulgarity of the city's common people. She might turn up her nose and demand to be taken home.

Or she might have changed her mind already, he thought as the carriage drew up in Russell Square. He'd not blame her. Only a hint of grey in the eastern sky suggested that dawn was on its way.

He stepped out and looked up at the façade. In one window a curtain was twitched aside momentarily, the fabric blue in a glow of lamplight.

Billy appeared at his elbow. "I went to the kitching door, guv, and knocked up the scullery maid; and sent 'er to wake miss's abigail wiv your letter. Will I ring the bell now?"

"No, we'll wait."

After a brief interval the fanlight above the front door brightened. The door opened and a figure in a shabby blue cloak slipped out. The door closed.

For a disappointed moment, Rod thought Thea had sent her maid to say she would not go. Then he realized that the figure was Thea herself. He stepped forward.

"Miss Kilmore, where is your abigail?"

"She cannot come. At least, Penny has more need of her than I. It turns out she has a trick that eases the discomfort of... of—"

"Morning sickness? Did we not agree that you could speak freely to me?"

"Yes, sir, so I will say that whatever you and Mama may think, I am past the age to need a chaperon. Pray do not tell me we cannot go."

"Very well, I shall not." Laughing, he handed her into the carriage. He seated himself opposite, knocked to direct the coachman to drive on, then said seriously, "All the same, you really must not go about in public without a female companion, or at least one of your brother's footmen."

"By 'in public' you mean where I might be seen by the ton, do you not? I begin to think it unlikely that we shall ever enter polite circles."

"Why is that?" he asked, dismayed.

"Jason says that Mama must introduce us to Society's hostesses, but she is not acquainted with any. For myself, it does not matter, but my sister longs to make her come-out." Thea took a deep breath, which Rod was coming to recognize as her way of steeling herself to accomplish some task she found alarming. "I don't suppose you know any lady who might be willing to take Meg under her wing?"

"I will see what I can do," he said, more curtly than he had intended. He was aware of a certain disillusionment. Like every other female, Miss Thea Kilmore was after what she could get from him, even if it was for her sister, not herself.

His tone made her wince. She seemed on the point of saying something, then decided against it.

The carriage rolled south. As the day advanced, the streets grew busier with coal carts, brewers' drays, apprentices opening shop fronts, and maids chatting while they scrubbed doorsteps. In silence, Thea watched the activity through the carriage window, her sensitive mouth drooping.

Rod could not bear her quiet despondency. "I am sorry for snapping at you," he said. "It was unfair when I had just told you to speak your mind frankly."

She turned to him eagerly. "Oh no, it was my fault for trespassing on your kindness. Indeed, I would have apologized and withdrawn my request, but for Meg's sake I was willing to brave your displeasure."

"You are a devoted sister."

"Until Jason brought Penny to Newkirk, Meg was my only friend," she said simply. "I want to see her happily married, perhaps the more so because I shall not wed."

"You are determined against marriage?"

"I am trying to be realistic. At twenty-five, I must be considered on the shelf even were I not too tall and too stupidly timid to attract a husband. Megan is pretty and lively, and her youthful charm may be expected to offset her lack of fortune. I believe she can make a respectable match—with the proper introductions and fashionable clothes."

"I daresay she will," he conceded.

He would have gone on to dispute her poor opinion of her own attractions, but she said anxiously, "Penny bought me a beautiful new pelisse, but I thought, considering where we are going, that I'd best wear my old cloak. I hope you are not offended that I did not dress in my best to go with you."

Smiling, he shook his head. "My dear Miss Kilmore, I am not so easily offended. Your cloak is altogether suitable for the market. I wish I had had the same thought. I fear I shall stand out like a chaffinch among sparrows."

"Not a chaffinch, a pheasant." She clapped her hand to her mouth in dismay at where the licence granted her tongue had led her, but above her hand her eyes twinkled at him.

He laughed. "Come now, I am not so very much larger than my fellows, any more than you are. It is the constant contrast with your mother and sister that makes you over-conscious of your height."

She gave him a look at once grateful and doubting. He had no time to reinforce his point, for the carriage came to a halt and Billy opened the door.

The noise of the market struck their ears. Cries of "'Taties, fine 'taties," and "Buy my white cauliflower," mingled with arguments over prices, a baby's wail, and a general rumble of business and gossip.

Rod helped Thea down and settled her hand firmly on his arm. "Don't stray," he commanded, and she nodded, overwhelmed by the bustling turmoil.

The crowd parted instinctively before the tall aristocrat, and Thea and the marquis wandered between barrows, barrels, baskets, crates and cartloads of carrots and cabbages and celery. The pungency of homegrown leeks and onions mingled with the fragrance of oranges and lemons from Malta and Majorca. A display of broccoli took Thea's interest.

"I wonder if that is the Roman or Neapolitan," she whispered to Rod. "It does not look quite like either."

"I haven't the least notion! You must ask the stall holder."

"Oh no, I could not speak to her."

"She does appear to be something of a shrew."

The woman was roundly abusing a man who had complained that half her stock was wilted. However, she answered Rod's question civilly enough, with a positive flood of information about the cultivation of broccoli.

Thanking her, he turned to Thea. "Most of that was beyond me. Was it of any use to you?"

"Most helpful. At Newkirk I was never able to obtain the varieties I read about, but I shall try to find seed while I am here. You see, one can have a supply throughout the winter if one plants the right kinds at the right time."

He listened to her earnest exposition, impressed with her knowledge and enthusiasm. Unladylike, perhaps, but of vastly more practical use than embroidery or playing upon the harp.

"How came you to your interest?" he asked.

She flushed. "I know it is not a suitable occupation for a lady. I started because our gardener died, and someone had to feed the family. At Newkirk we have only what we produce ourselves. I enjoyed growing things and wanted to learn more, so I ordered books on kitchen gardening from the lending library. The library at Carlisle is sadly limited and out of date, which is why I am still shockingly ignorant."

"You seem to me to know a great deal." Touched by pity for the hand-to-mouth existence led by the Kilmore ladies in Northumberland, he recalled with anger the carefree life of Jason Kilmore and his late father in London.

They moved on. Several times Thea stopped with questions, but she avoided directly addressing the market people, even a motherly-looking woman with a basket of mulberries. Rod guessed that she was simply shy with strangers, but the regrettable example of his mother was too clear in his mind. The Marchioness of Hazlewood considered a large proportion of the Polite World beneath her notice. Was it possible Thea felt likewise about the stall-holder?

Thea pointed out to him a barrow laden with five or six different sorts of apples. The ferret-faced man behind it noticed. With a broken-toothed grin, he polished a russet-hued apple on his grimy sleeve and held it out to her.

"Want a taste, ducky?"

She hesitated. Rod was about to intervene when he saw a small hand creep up from beneath the barrow and seize one of the largest apples.

The man pounced. "Gotcha." He hauled out a ragged, shoeless urchin and yelled for a beadle.

The child, a boy of about ten, whimpered in his grasp. A few onlookers gathered, but the sight was too commonplace to attract much attention.

A stout constable pushed through the unheeding crowd.

"Don' give me to 'im, guv," the boy begged, tears streaking his dirty face. "I'll do anyfing. I'll work for nuffing. My sister'll die if I—"

"Shut yer gob, you dirty little thief," the barrow man snarled, shaking him. "I got a living to make. Here, orficer, here's anuvver bloody Newgate bird for yer."

Rod stepped forward. "Just a minute. What was that you said about your sister, lad?"

The boy clutched at his sleeve. "She's sick, yer 'onner, and starving. Wivout me, she won't last the day. She's only little."

"You don't want to believe a word of it, sir," said the constable pompously, licking his pencil. "Lie as easy as they breathe, they do. 'Anging's too good for 'em." He turned to the apple-seller. "I'll take 'im off your 'ands now but you'll 'ave to come round to the public office in Bow Street later to swear a warrant. Name?"

"Wait," Rod interrupted. "I doubt he's an incorrigible villain and I've a mind to enquire further into this matter. I'll stand surety for the boy. I am the Marquis of Hazlewood and you may find me in Arlington Street, St. James's."

"Yes, my lord. Certainly, my lord." The constable wrote laboriously in his notebook. "What's your name, boy?"

"Peter Barker. I don' 'ave to go to gaol?"

"Long as you stays out o' trouble, young fella-me-lad. If you goes pinching stuff again, you'll be 'anged and 'is lordship 'ere'll 'ave to pay. You mind what 'is lordship tells you."

"Oy, what abaht me apple?" demanded the barrow man, unimpressed.

"I'll pay you for the apple and I'll take a dozen more." Rod dropped a shilling into the man's outstretched palm.

"'Elp yerself, m'lord, and if yer wants my advice, keep yer 'and on that young bugger or 'e'll scarper."

Rod put a couple of apples in each pocket of his topcoat and, at his gesture, the wide-eyed boy stuffed the rest into his pockets and torn shirt-front.

"Can I give one to my sister?"

"If she really exists, you may give them all to her. Where is she?"

Peter pointed south, towards the river, and started eagerly in that direction. About to follow, Rod suddenly remembered Thea. He glanced around. She was standing a few feet behind him, a look of helpless distress on her face. She had every right to take him to task for deserting her.

"My apologies, Miss Kilmore. I shall have to take you back to the carriage and send you home without my escort, I fear."

"Let me come with you," she begged, to his surprise. "If the little girl is ill, you must not waste any time finding her."

"Peter's home is undoubtedly no fit place for a lady."

"I shall be safe with you. But I do think we should buy some bread and milk if she is truly starving. Apples are not very digestible."

He took her hand and pressed it. "A good thought. Come, then."

As they turned towards Southampton Street, Rod made no attempt to restrain Peter. If the boy were lying, he would make his escape, continue thieving, and eventually be caught and suffer the penalty. If he were telling the truth, he had no reason to run off.

Peter stuck close to his side, now and then touching his sleeve as if to be sure he was really there. "Rosie's all I got," he confided. "Me mam died when she was born, then not too long ago Pa got bit by a prancer and 'is 'and swelled up somefing awful and 'e died. 'E were an ostler. I could've joined a flash 'ouse gang and been took care of, but they wouldn't 'ave Rosie acos she's too little to prig stuff or—" he glanced at Thea "—or anyfing."

"So you tried thievery on your own account." Rod kept the judgement from his voice. For abandoned children, the choices were all too few.

"Not till I 'ad to! I've swep' crossings and 'eld 'orses, but sometimes you 'old a gentleman's 'orses and then 'e don't give you nuffing. I could've got by if it was just me, but I got Rosie to look after."

His fierce loyalty to his little sister reminded Rod of Thea's protectiveness towards Megan and Penny. He had sisters of his own, both older and younger, but they had never needed more than his occasional escort. His philanthropy had turned outwards.

Now, however, his thoughts turned to the inner man as the smell of new bread wafted to his nostrils. He had left home without breakfasting.

"There is a baker's shop," said Thea.

"Will you go in, Miss Kilmore?" He didn't want to leave either her or the boy alone outside. "Buy what you think appropriate for the children, and add a little something for me."

She flushed. "I did not bring any money, sir."

"My dear girl, you must never go out without at least a shilling for a hackney," he reproved her, digging in his pocket for change. The apples were in the way. He gave one to Peter, saying, "Eat," and sank his teeth into another as Thea disappeared into the shop.

Nothing was left but two cores by the time she came out with a large loaf, three meat pasties, and a small tin can with a cover and a wire handle. "Milk," she explained. "I had to buy the can, too, but I thought you would not mind."

"I'll carry it, miss," Peter volunteered.

She passed it to him, along with one of the pasties, and gave another to Rod. "Would it be very unladylike in me to eat in the street?" she asked uncertainly.

Rod suppressed a sudden, unaccountable urge to hug her. "I would not encourage you to walk down Bond Street nibbling on a hot meat pie. Here, I simply advise you to take off your gloves first."

Laughing, she complied.

As they swallowed the last bites of piecrust, Peter led them off the Strand into a warren of tenements separated by tiny, dingy courts. He turned into a crooked alley so narrow they had to walk in single file.

On either side blank brick walls rose to a few small windows on the first-floor level. Overhanging eaves high above admitted a mere streak of grey daylight to the airless, dankly cold ravine. Following Thea, Rod cursed himself for letting her come. It was the perfect place for a trap, with no room for him to use his advantages of strength and reach. At least he ought to have had the sense to wear old clothes, as she had, so as not to attract greedy eyes.

He was about to call a halt to the enterprise when they turned a corner and came to the blind, rubbish-filled end of the alley.

"Rosie?"

Half hidden by a broken crate, a bundle of rags stirred. Thea darted forward and took the filthy, shivering child in her arms. Too late to warn of the danger of typhus fever, Rod could only think how wrong he had been to compare her to his mother.

CHAPTER SEVEN

"So Peter will be Hazlewood's new tiger, and Rosie is to live with a family at his country seat in Buckinghamshire. He spends at least half the year there, so they will see each other often. I told him he must not separate them more than he can help." Reaching the end of her story, Thea realized that her mother was more worried than approving. Her excitement ebbed and she sank wearily onto one of the new Chippendale chairs.

"Oh dear, it was scarcely proper in you to instruct the marquis, my love."

"He did not take it amiss, Mama. We are friends."

"Friendship seldom leads to warmer feelings," Meg informed her knowledgeably. "To make him fall in love, you must dress in your best and flirt with him, not wear your old cloak and rush around rescuing ragamuffins."

"I have not the knack of flirting, and even if I had, Lord Hazlewood is not in the least likely to fall in love with me."

"No, I suppose not. Jason says he is very rich and grand—the *crème de la crème!*—and much sought after, but he has never paid his addresses even to the most beautiful and eligible young ladies. Not that he is either a rake or a recluse. He goes to all the best balls and parties, and Almack's, and is generally regarded as a paragon of propriety."

"Then I cannot think what he was about, Thea," the dowager fretted, "to involve you in such an unpleasant business. Does he suppose you so lost to all sense of decorum that anything is acceptable? I fear you started on the wrong foot with him, at that inn, and then to go out this morning without your maid!"

"I'm sorry, Mama," Thea murmured impenitently. She would not have missed this morning for the world, and Farden's daunting presence would have spoiled it.

"I ought not to have allowed you to go to Covent Garden at all. You must behave with particular care in future and hope that time will erase the unfortunate impression."

"Yes, Mama." In theory she agreed. She suspected, though, that if she showed herself to be a conventional, demure young lady, she would forfeit the warm regard he had expressed after their adventure. She'd fade into insignificance among a crowd of sophisticated beauties; for, as they parted, he had promised once again to smooth the Kilmores' path into Society.

In Society, alas, she knew she would be as tongue-tied as ever. She reserved the right to enjoy without qualms the indulgent friendship Lord Hazlewood offered.

LADY HAZLEWOOD opened her eyes as her son entered her sitting-room. Reclining on a chaise longue, heavy-eyed, she presented a picture of fragility, her natural pallor accentuated by the plum-coloured watered silk she favoured. With a languid gesture, she raised one thin hand for Rod to kiss.

"Roderick, dearest," she said and sighed. "I fear my nerves are so debilitated at present I find myself unable to concentrate on even Bishop Porteus's estimable sermons."

Retrieving the book that lay on the floor by her couch, open and face down, one page crumpled, Rod glanced at the title. *Château du Mystère, ou Adolphe et Eugénie.* "Porteus was an admirable preacher," he said gravely, restoring it to her. If his mother wished to pretend that the latest French novel was a book of sermons, who was he to contradict her?

He looked around for a seat and as usual decided to stand. His mother's fashionably spindly furniture always made him very much aware of his bulk. He crossed to the exquisite Adam fireplace and warmed his hands.

"I daresay the hurly-burly of London is responsible for your irritated nerves," he went on. "Perhaps your health would profit from a return to the country."

She sat bolt upright. "The country? At this season? Nothing could be worse, I assure you. As for hurly-burly, on the contrary, London is somewhat thin of company at present. Though it is shocking how many mushrooms have the impertinence to suppose that one might honour their assemblies with one's presence. Naturally one does not respond to such effrontery. Had you something particular to say to me, Roderick?"

"Yes, Mother. Since London is thin of company, you will be glad to hear that I wish to bring a family of ladies to call when you are next at home."

"Ladies with whom I am unacquainted?" she asked sceptically.

"You may, perhaps, have some past acquaintance with the Dowager Lady Kilmore, though she has not frequented Society these many years."

"The late Baron Kilmore's relict? No, I never met her, and I have no desire to rectify the omission. Kilmore was a ne'er-do-well, and his son is a thoroughgoing scoundrel. Did he not run off with Trevelyan's wife?''

''Yes,'' Rod admitted, ''if the tattlemongers are to be believed. Though of course she was not yet his wife at the time.''

''It is all very well for you to disapprove of gossip, but there is no smoke without a flame. You cannot expect me to countenance such immorality by receiving Kilmore's family. Dowager, you said? I suppose he has ensnared some vulgar heiress in his toils.''

''The new Lady Kilmore is a lawyer's daughter, but she is perfectly presentable.''

''And she has cozened you into insinuating her into the ton.''

''I have seen very little of Lady Kilmore,'' said Rod coolly. ''It is Kilmore's sisters who hope to make their bow to Society. Their birth is impeccable and they are not to blame for their father's and brother's indiscretions.''

''I might have guessed this was no more than your latest quixotic start,'' Lady Hazlewood said with contempt. ''You will have to apply to someone else to rescue the Kilmores from the effects of their disgraced name.''

''You mistake me, madam.'' He let a hint of steel enter his voice. ''I said I wish to bring the ladies to call upon you, but in fact that is my unalterable intention. Unless you prefer to retire to the dower house at the castle, they will attend your at home next Friday.''

''Yorkshire! I told you my nerves will not stand a sojourn in the country at this season.'' She sank back against her cushions, her eyes closed, her hands clasped to her heart. ''Oh, I can feel a spasm coming on. Call Wilkins at once! My vinaigrette!''

Rod rang for her abigail, but he was unimpressed by her theatrical collapse. He had discovered many years ago that Lady Hazlewood's vinaigrette contained sugar crystals, as sal volatile made her sneeze. Her nervous spasms only attacked when she was thwarted, and were soonest cured by calm and firmness.

"I shall convey your invitation to the Kilmores," he said as Wilkins rushed in.

"On no account!" She would have sat up again, had not the abigail been waving the small cut-glass bottle under her nose. "I hope I know my duty," she went on faintly. "*I* shall send an invitation."

He thanked her as courteously as if it had been her own notion to entertain his friends. As he took his leave, he cast a silent blessing upon the ancestor who had built a mansion in Bucks and converted the old Yorkshire manor house near the medieval castle ruins into a comfortable—and distant—dower house.

Nonetheless, as always, a confrontation with his mother left an unpleasant taste in his mouth. He decided to drive out to the neat little villa in Hampstead where Sue's undemanding company would soon restore his peace of mind. For years now her quiet common sense had been as important to him as the services she rendered as his mistress. She, if anyone, would understand that he could not leave an unworldly innocent like Thea Kilmore to struggle unaided for her family's welfare.

On his way out to his curricle, Rod met Will in the vestibule. As his heir presumptive, his cousin had apartments in the Hazlewood Town house, though he was well able to afford lodgings, or even a modest house, of his own. He came and went as he pleased, his carefree light-heartedness relieving the formal atmosphere of the place. Yet his manners were punctilious enough to satisfy his exacting aunt.

"I hear you have a new tiger," Will said in greeting. "You've been rushing to the rescue again, eh? Miss Kilmore cannot say enough of your good deeds."

"You have been back to Russell Square? Take care or you will lose your reputation as a high stickler."

"On the contrary, coz, I daresay, if I chose, I could make even Bloomsbury fashionable. Care to wager?"

"Lord, no. You might succeed, but it would take a lifetime. It will be quicker to bring the Kilmores to the ton than the ton to Bloomsbury. They are to come here on Friday."

"To her ladyship's at home? Playing St. George again, are you?"

"Who is to take the dragon's rôle, Society or my mother?"

"Oh, Aunt Hazlewood, beyond a doubt, in her own inimitable way. I know you can deal with her, but I'll be damned if I dare cross her. They'll need all the support they can get. I'll be there, and you can return the favour by coming with us to Kew. It's all arranged for tomorrow, weather permitting. I've invited Uncle Reggie along to do the pretty to the dowager."

"Good gad, that old court-card?"

"You are speaking of my relative, I'd remind you." Will drew himself up, attempting to look offended, then relaxed and grinned. "Yes, that old court-card. I couldn't think of anyone else who would not object to Russell Square. For all he's Prinny's bosom beau, he's been in Queer Street often enough to find anything short of the Fleet a respectable address."

"Consorting with the Prince Regent has left many a man with pockets to let. So he goes with us to entertain the dowager, and what of Lady Kilmore?"

"I couldn't very well cut her out of the invitation, but with luck she will be indisposed."

Rod frowned. "Apart from that unfortunate elopement, her conduct seems unexceptionable. Certainly the other ladies regard her as one of them, and whatever her antecedents, she is now a baroness. I believe it will not do to exclude her."

"All the same, one can hope that her delicate condition will prevail," Will pointed out. "Your horses are waiting, coz. Where are you off to?"

"Hampstead."

"My compliments to Mistress Susan. Don't forget, Kew tomorrow."

ONLY THE WEATHER cooperated with Will's hopes for the expedition. First, Penelope Kilmore was well enough to go. Then, the Honourable Reginald Glubb-ffoulkes, instead of doing his duty by the dowager, took a fancy to Miss Megan.

Will's Uncle Reggie was a stout, florid gentleman whose high, starched shirt points and cravat made it impossible for him to nod or turn his head. Instead, he would incline the upper part of his body, resulting in a curious creaking.

"My Cumberland corset," he explained, quite without embarrassment. "An excellent device made popular, among gentlemen of substantial girth, by my friend the Regent."

Meg giggled. Wheezing, he chucked her under the chin, called her a naughty puss, and refused to be detached from her side. Will was forced to attend the dowager as they strolled about the Royal Botanic Garden.

Though Mr. DeVine politely concealed his disappointment, Thea saw the occasional frustrated glances he cast her giggling sister's way. She sympathized with his frustration. She had hoped to talk to Lord Hazlewood, but Penny needed the support of his strong arm, and he seemed bent on furthering his acquaintance with her. Not that he ignored Thea; he included her in the conversation, and when she expressed an interest, he found a gardener to explain to her the cultivation of oranges, lemons and pineapples. She chided herself for coveting the marquis's undivided attention.

When they returned to Russell Square, Penny civilly invited the gentlemen to step in for refreshments. Mr. Glubb-ffoulkes, whose animation had begun to flag, brightened, and he accepted with alacrity.

Lord Hazlewood and Mr. DeVine also accepted. Penny led the way into the drawing-room, now furnished in the sturdy, comfortable, yet elegant style of Thomas Chippendale. The new butler, Dunmow, treading with measured dignity, brought tea, wine and cakes. His last position had been as upper-footman and he was very anxious to prove himself. He poured wine for the gentlemen and passed the cakes, of which Mr. Glubb-ffoulkes partook liberally with every evidence of delight. Seated as close to the tea table as his pent-in paunch allowed, he congratulated his hostess on her cook.

"I recall what you told me of your previous cook's way with an egg," Lord Hazlewood said to Thea with a smile. "If the present cook is so great an improvement, Lady Kilmore must be accounted a competent judge of servants. Is she also responsible for the decoration of this room? It is charming."

"Is it not?" Thea looked round the room, admiring again the soothing sage green and ivory enlivened by touches of russet, enjoying the quiet luxury after the faded shabbiness of Newkirk. "Penny has excellent taste."

"So I am discovering. You will pardon my frankness—since I have given you leave to be frank with me—if I say I marvel to find such refinement of taste in one of her background."

"Mama cannot quite believe it," she confided. "Of course, Penny did attend a ladies' seminary."

"So she mentioned. What is more, her father was not a merchant, but a lawyer who had many great families as his clients."

"She acted as his hostess after she left school."

"That explains her self-possession. She is a lady in every way but birth and will be less of a detriment to your sister's chances than I had feared."

"I am so glad." Relieved and gratified, Thea smiled across the room at Penny. Her answering smile was weary. Beside her, Will's uncle reached for the last slice of plum cake. "No wonder Mr. Glubb-ffoulkes needs a corset! I believe it is time I rescued Penny from him. She is looking tired and ought to retire."

Penny gratefully ceded her place at the tea tray. "I'll order more cake and biscuits," she said, and slipped out of the room.

"A fine figure of a woman," Mr. Glubb-ffoulkes observed, "not but what she ain't as lively as your little sister, ma'am."

Thea had no notion what to say. She in turn was rescued by Lord Hazlewood. He came to join them and asked the ageing dandy if it were true that Prinny had gone off to Suffolk with the Hertfords although Princess Charlotte's baby was due any day.

"Gone shooting," he confirmed. "Never fear, he'll come rushing back when the moment comes. Fond of the chit, he is, for all she takes after her mother with her hoydenish ways."

"Lese-majesty," said the marquis, pretending to be shocked.

"Gammon, my boy, just quoting Prinny himself. Aha, here comes . . . oh." He ended on a note of disappointment as he saw that the butler bore a silver salver with a calling-card, instead of the expected plate of cakes.

His stately mien marred by a trace of excitement, Dunmow approached the dowager, bowed low, and presented the salver. "The Marchioness of Hazlewood, my lady," he announced, his impressive tone indicating that gentlemen callers were all very well in their way, but it was the ladies who counted.

"Your mama, Hazlewood?" The dowager took the card and studied it with an air of perplexity. "Surely you have not kept the marchioness waiting outside, Dunmow?"

"Certainly not, my lady," he said, offended. "Her ladyship sent her carriage and a footman. If your ladyship will turn the card over . . ."

"Thank you, Dunmow, that will be all." As he retreated, she did as he had suggested, and read aloud, "'At home, Friday. Lady Hazlewood requests the pleasure of the company of the Dowager Lady Kilmore and the Misses Kilmore.'"

"An invitation!" cried Meg. She turned to the marquis to ask, "This is your doing, sir? Thank you."

"I told my mother I meant to take you to call on her," he said, "and she offered to write an invitation, though she usually does not for an informal at home." To Thea, he sounded less than pleased.

"Nothing my aunt does is informal," Will contradicted. "I assure you, Miss Megan, Aunt Hazlewood is the highest stickler on the face of the earth. It comes of being a duke's daughter. It's a feather in your cap to get an invitation from her."

"Deuced high in the instep," confirmed Mr. Glubbffoulkes, with an anxious look at the door.

Their words increased Thea's suspicion. "Mama, may I see the card?" she requested.

Meg jumped up and brought it to her. "See, is it not splendid?"

Thea turned it over and read the quavery handwriting on the reverse. " 'The Dowager Lady Kilmore and the Misses Kilmore.' This deliberately excludes my sister-in-law, does it not, sir?" she asked Lord Hazlewood, praying that he had not arranged matters thus.

"I'm afraid so. I ought to have anticipated this, but I promise you I did not."

The only thing Thea could think of worse than vexing Lord Hazlewood and his mother was deserting Penny. She took a deep breath. "If Penny cannot go, we shall not accept."

"But we must, Thea!" Meg was horrified. "Penny will not mind. She is not well enough to gad about."

"Better go, Miss Kilmore." Mr. Glubb-ffoulkes spoke without removing his mournful gaze from the empty cake plate. "Don't want to offend Lady Hazlewood. Ah, that's more like it," he added as Dunmow came in to replace the distressing object with a full plate and to refill his glass. Mr. Glubb-ffoulkes retired from the discussion.

"All too easy to offend my aunt," Will agreed. "Half the ton is in her black books."

"I do think we ought to go, Thea," her mother said in her soft, doubtful voice. "It may be difficult to come by another invitation if we refuse."

"We should not be here at all if it were not for Penny," Thea pointed out in distress. "If she cannot go, I shall not."

"Well, I shall," Meg declared. "My lord, will Lady Hazlewood be affronted if Thea does not go with us?"

"I scarcely think you need worry about displeasing my mother, Miss Megan. As Will so elegantly phrases it, half the ton is in her black books, so her disapproval will not affect your standing with them. However, I have no intention of excluding Lady Kilmore from my home. I shall be here at three o'clock on Friday, expecting to convey four ladies to Arlington Street."

Thea's heart swelled with gratitude. How could she have doubted him for a moment? As always, he had extricated her from her predicament with a few words. What need of a fairy godmother when the Marquis of Hazlewood was at hand?

The only trouble, she suddenly realized, was that she would have been glad of an excuse not to go.

CHAPTER EIGHT

THE LOOKING-GLASS reflected the image of a slender, fashionable young lady in a high-waisted pelisse of lavender blue velvet, lined and trimmed with white satin. Thea gazed at herself in wonder. Perhaps, after all, she was only three inches too tall, not six as she had always supposed.

"Your hat, miss," said Farden, handing her a French bonnet of the same materials. "You was quite right, miss, if you'll pardon the liberty, to choose the silk flowers. Feathers'd look top-heavy, like, you being so nice and slim."

"Thank you, Farden." Thea smiled at the abigail. No longer a stranger, she seemed less intimidating, and her approval was a comfort. Meg had argued that ostrich plumes were *de rigueur,* but Penny, though she herself settled for a curling plume, had supported Thea's choice.

She set the bonnet on her head, tied the wide ribbons, and turned back to the mirror. No one at Lady Hazlewood's could take exception to her appearance, she decided. All she had to do was hold her tongue and she would scrape through safely.

"Thea, are you ready?" Meg pattered in, her face aglow with excitement beneath her deep rose hat with its three nodding plumes. "Lord Hazlewood should be here at any moment. Mama and Penny have already gone down. Penny is wearing the Russian cloak with the sable trim. I wish I had one like it."

"My dear, you would disappear from view."

"Or at least look as wide as I am tall, I daresay," Meg agreed gaily. "Penny looks positively queenly in it. I cannot see how the marchioness can possibly object to her. Here are your gloves. Do come."

She ran ahead and reached the drawing-room before Thea, pulling on her gloves, was halfway down the stairs. The doorbell rang. Dunmow, lying in wait, swung the door open to admit a blast of raw, damp air and Lord Hazlewood.

Taking off his hat, the marquis caught sight of Thea. His eyes widened. With a smile he came forward and gave her his hand as she descended the last step. "The picture of elegance," he said. "That shade suits you admirably."

She willed the heat to recede from her cheeks. His kind compliment was designed to relieve the nervousness he had guessed at, not to agitate her further. "We are all dressed in our best, sir," she assured him. Extricating her hand from his clasp, which was as perturbing as his words, she preceded him towards the drawing-room. "We do not wish to put you to the blush. Mama and Penny have been tutoring Meg and me in the proper behaviour. You need not fear I shall say anything untoward."

"The possibility was far from my mind, Miss Kilmore. I know you venture to speak only under the direst necessity."

The friendly, teasing note in his voice reminded her of the way he quizzed his cousin and set her at ease far more effectively than any number of compliments. "I hope I speak only when I have something to say," she retorted.

"Ah, that is quite different," he said, laughing. "If only everyone would observe so sensible a restriction."

Meg heard him and came out of the drawing-room, followed by her mother and Penny. "We are all ready," she said eagerly. "Shall we go?"

He started back in mock surprise. "Ready? Miss Megan, you must learn to keep gentlemen waiting. It is expected of a pretty young lady."

"What a shocking waste of time." She gave him a saucy look. "Besides, lateness may be expected, but I doubt it is appreciated. *I* shall not strive to be always late."

"With luck you will set a fashion. Let us waste no time, then, but be on our way."

He had provided hot bricks in his carriage for the ladies' feet, and warm rugs for their knees. Thea sat beside him, their backs to the horses, facing the other three. As they rumbled through the streets towards St. James's, he described the people they were likely to meet in his mother's drawing-room.

"First, there are her cronies, ladies who agree with her opinion of the decay of modern manners and morals. Mrs. Venables always attends, and Lady Fetherstonehaugh, and sometimes the Duchess of Trent. Then there are the leaders of Society, including the patronesses of Almack's, who go to show each other they are still received by the Marchioness of Hazlewood. Her assemblies are much more exclusive than Almack's, you see."

"I hope I shall get vouchers for Almack's when the Season starts," said Meg hopefully. "Mama, pray cultivate the acquaintance of the patronesses."

The dowager looked alarmed. "Vouchers depend as much on unexceptionable conduct as on knowing the patronesses," she reminded her daughter.

The third factor, of course, was lineage. Thea knew that Penny was sure her birth barred her from the august portals. To be sure, Lady Jersey was the granddaughter of a banker, yet—perhaps for that reason—she was known as the most particular of all the lady patronesses. Thea would not go without Penny, but Meg had set her heart on attending the Marriage Mart and ought to be able to do so.

"I have every intention of conducting myself with propriety," Meg said with dignity. "Who else will be there today, sir?"

"Mother tells me company is thin, but I daresay there will be a few matrons presenting daughters to her in hopes of winning the cachet of invitations to her entertainments."

"No gentlemen?"

"There are always a few, escorting the ladies." The marquis sounded amused. "Never fear, Miss Megan, Will has promised to turn up, though he generally avoids such occasions like the plague. No doubt he feels you will be glad to see a familiar face."

"*I* certainly shall," Thea admitted.

"A room full of strangers can be disconcerting." He smiled at her, then added with a hint of embarrassment, "I ought to advise you not to be disconcerted if my mother appears to be ailing. Her health is much better than she clai . . . believes."

Meg opened her mouth to question him, but at that moment the carriage turned between tall wrought-iron gates and came to a halt in a courtyard before a porticoed mansion. Thea gazed at it in awe as Lord Hazlewood handed Penny down. Most Town houses had nothing but railings and a sunken area separating them from the pavement. She had not realized that the Hazlewoods' house would be so grand.

Stepping down in turn, she took Penny's hand and pressed it. "It is very impressive, is it not?" she whispered. "You have not said a word this age. Does the prospect of facing the ton for the first time terrify you as it does me?"

"I should not mind it if only Jason were beside me." She hugged her cloak about her.

Meg joined them. "What a splendid house! It is almost a palace. No wonder everyone hopes for an invitation."

The marquis led the way inside. Will met them in the vestibule, an octagonal chamber with a chequered floor of black-and-white marble, lit by a clerestory window below the domed ceiling. On the far side rose a wide staircase of white marble, with gilt balusters. Several double doors led off the hall, separated by niches containing marble statuary. Thea found the effect chilling.

Meg was unawed. After one glance at Will, dressed today in a black-and-grey striped coat, pale grey pantaloons, and a richly pink satin waistcoat, she giggled.

"You look like a bullfinch, Mr. DeVine."

"Dash it, do I? And after I rejected brown and scarlet because they made me look like a robin redbreast!"

"An excessively smart bullfinch."

He grinned at her. "That's all right, then."

"Birds of a feather," Lord Hazlewood pointed out, indicating Meg's pink plumes. Aided by butler and footman, he divested himself of hat, gloves, and overcoat, emerging in a sober blue coat and cream marcella waistcoat.

With an encouraging smile for Thea, he offered a crooked arm each to her mother and Penny, while Will gravely did the same for Thea and Meg. Two more footmen in olive-green-and-silver livery opened the nearest pair of doors.

Since the master of the house accompanied the ladies, the butler did not announce them. The marquis advanced into the room. Over her mother's head, Thea saw a long salon with tall, damask-curtained windows along one side. The predominant colours were eau-de-Nil, ivory, and gilt, with a profusion of intricate ormolu. Cabinets decorated with painted medallions, Grecian urns on pedestals, and fanciful plasterwork added to the elaborate ornateness of the décor. Delicate Adam chairs and sofas, scattered in small groups, were occupied by ladies of all ages, from whom rose a subdued murmur of conversation.

Amidst the flock of nodding plumes, one lady in a dainty cap of Malines lace dominated the room. Her dark purple gown drew attention to the purple shadows around her sunken eyes. Thea thought she looked alarmingly ill, whatever the marquis said, and wondered why she was entertaining. As they approached, however, she saw that Lady Hazlewood's eyes, far from displaying the suffering of an invalid, gleamed with fury. In fact, they darted venom at her son.

"Lady Kilmore, Mother," said the marquis urbanely, "and the Dowager Lady Kilmore."

Inclining her head a fraction of an inch, Lady Hazlewood said to the dowager in a faint voice, "How do you do, ma'am." Her gaze turned to Penny. She shuddered, sank back weakly with closed eyes, and murmured to the stout matron in lilac silk at her side, "My smelling salts, Hortense, if you will be so good."

Thea's mother gasped something incoherent.

"How do you do, ma'am," said Penny coolly, as if she had not been given the cut direct. Thea was proud of her.

A second crony of the marchioness's, on her other side, gave Penny an appraising stare and then allowed a faint smile of approval to appear. "I am acquainted with your husband, Lady Kilmore," she said.

"Her grace of Trent." Lord Hazlewood hastened to make the introduction.

Further words were exchanged, but Thea did not catch them. It was her and Meg's turn to face the marchioness.

"Miss Kilmore and Miss Megan, Aunt," said Will.

They curtsied. Without opening her eyes, Lady Hazlewood gave a feeble wave of the hand, apparently intended to serve as both greeting and dismissal.

As the others had moved on, Will presented Thea and Meg to the duchess, who acknowledged the introduction with an air of boredom. He hustled them onwards.

"Deuced bad ton," he said disapprovingly. "Rod may have forced my aunt to receive Lady Kilmore, but that's no excuse for out-and-out rudeness. I'll apologize if Rod hasn't."

"Pray don't, Mr. DeVine," Thea begged. "To remark upon Lady Hazlewood's incivility can only increase Penny's discomfort."

"You have a point there. Best not draw attention to it. By Jove, but she carried it off well, didn't she? As if she had moved in the First Circles all her life. Oh, there's Giddy Turner. He complained the other evening that his mother was making him squire yet a husband-hunting sister. Come on, I'll introduce you."

Thea saw a lanky young man leaning against the wall, half hidden by an urn. In front of him, a bran-faced young lady and her mother sat with rigid spines on the edge of their seats, their expressions masks of polite attention. Opposite them sat another mother and daughter, equally stiff, the elder making some remark that appeared to be of no great interest to anyone.

Either they were all as starchy as the marchioness, Thea decided, or their excessive decorum was designed to curry her favour. In either case, they had probably noticed how she snubbed the Kilmores and would take their lead from her. Thea did not want to face them.

Feeling cowardly, she retreated to her mother's side, while Meg went off happily with Will. The oddly named Giddy Turner brightened as Will approached, and within a few minutes the whole group was chatting with animated faces. Meg's cheerful laugh made heads turn.

Near the window, Lord Hazlewood and Penny were talking to a dark, pretty woman of about thirty. She must have taken her cue from the Duchess of Trent rather than the marchioness.

"Do you know who that is, Mama?" Thea asked.

"Lady Cowper. Hazlewood offered to make me known to her, of course, but I was afraid..."

"I know, so was I. But she must be perfectly amiable if she is talking to Penny after Lady Hazlewood was so odious."

"Emily Cowper is one of the patronesses, Thea. In the circumstances, I thought it best not to approach her here. I don't know how Penny can put herself forward like that. She may ruin Meg's chances."

"Oh, fustian, Mama! I beg your pardon, but Penny cannot be called forward when it was the marquis who made her acquainted with Lady Cowper. He himself has said there is nothing to blush for in her manners.''

At that moment a tall, thin, elderly lady approached them in a flutter of lilac gauze draperies. Even her cap had fluttering lilac ribbons, contrasting oddly with shrewd blue eyes and an eagle's beak of a nose. Her lack of outdoor clothes proclaimed her a resident of the house.

"You are Lady Kilmore," she announced. "Let me introduce myself, ma'am. Lady Anne DeVine, dear Roderick's aunt. How do you do, ma'am. And this is your daughter. Happy to make your acquaintance, Miss Kilmore."

Every statement issued disconcertingly from her lips as an announcement. Curtsying, Thea felt herself being scrutinized with uncommon astuteness, which might have been alarming had not Lady Anne proved her goodwill by the very act of speaking to them.

Having shaken the dowager's hand with a manly vigour, Lady Anne went on, "Do my best to avoid these nonsensical affairs of my sister-in-law's. Shocking waste of time, ma'am."

"My younger daughter..." bleated Lady Kilmore.

Lady Anne patted her shoulder sympathetically. "Different when there's a chit to be turned off. Can't be helped. Never married, myself."

The sound the dowager produced might have been commiseration; though, her husband having been what he was, it could also have been envy.

"I am a bluestocking, ma'am," Lady Anne declared with pride, raising the hem of her skirt to reveal bony ankles clad in cotton stockings of ultramarine blue. "I am engaged in translating a medical treatise from the German."

Nothing could have been better calculated to set the dowager at ease. For many years she had taken care of all the medical needs of tenants and neighbours in Newkirk and the surrounding area, the nearest apothecary being miles away. She was always eager to discover new cures. She and Lady Anne settled happily to a discussion of symptoms and treatments.

Left to her own devices, Thea watched the ebb and flow of guests in Lady Hazlewood's salon. The proper time for a call being no more than fifteen or twenty minutes, the marchioness was kept busy by a constant stream of greetings and farewells.

Lady Cowper departed, bowing and smiling as she passed Thea. Penny and the marquis came after her, but the marquis was waylaid en route by a ravishing blonde, who hung on his arm, gazing up into his eyes. With his invariable courtesy, he bent his head to listen to her with no sign of impatience. Why should he be impatient? Thea demanded of herself. Unable to think of a reason, she sighed. Any man would be flattered to have such a beauty casting such obvious lures at him.

Penny joined Thea. "Lady Cowper is prodigious good-natured," she reported. "If it were up to her alone, I might conceivably be admitted to Almack's. However, I thought it best not to request vouchers even for you and Meg. If they are not offered, someone of high social standing must approach the patronesses for you."

"Lord Hazlewood will," said Thea with confidence. "For Meg, at least. I do not care to go."

"Very wise, Miss Kilmore." Lady Anne had overheard. "A more insipid entertainment cannot be imagined." She nodded to Penny. "You must be the new Lady Kilmore. Don't let 'em frighten you, ma'am. A woman should be judged on her own merits, not her father's or her husband's."

Penny was nonplussed. While the dowager presented her in proper form, Thea turned her attention back to Lord Hazlewood. At that moment he gestured in her direction, his gaze on his beautiful companion. The blonde shook her head with a pettish frown, and glared after him as he deserted her to rejoin the Kilmores. Catching Thea's eye, the woman gave her a black scowl.

Thea guessed that she had refused to meet them. "I fear your friend is vexed," she said to the marquis when he reached her, after exchanging brief greetings with several of the people he passed.

"My friend?" he asked in surprise. "Oh, you mean Lady Daphne. A mere acquaintance."

"With ambitions to something warmer," said Will, coming up with Meg. "Like a dozen others, she has been setting her cap at Rod since she made her come-out, even, to my certain knowledge, refusing other offers. He's the greatest prize on the Town, you know."

"You flatter me, coz. Aunt Anne, I'm glad you managed to bring yourself to quit the library for a while. You are free to return thither now, since we must be leaving."

She beamed at him. "Anything, dear boy," she said obscurely. Turning to the dowager, she promised, "I'll hunt down that pamphlet for you, ma'am." With that, she rose and strode from the room, her extraordinary lilac draperies swirling.

"Aunt Anne has a mind above fashion," said Will mournfully.

Thea sprang to her defence. "She has a kind heart!"

"Well said." Lord Hazlewood smiled at her.

Meg's new acquaintances had already gone. Few of those now present had seen the Kilmores' arrival, but their departure was equally illuminating to anyone who cared for the marchioness's opinion. When Lord Hazlewood informed his mother that they were leaving, she waved her vinaigrette vaguely in their direction, then raised it to her nose and sniffed.

This time, following Penny's lead, they all took polite leave of her as if they had noticed nothing untoward in her behaviour. Thea thought she saw Lady Hazlewood's drooping mouth tighten for the merest instant.

Perhaps that was a victory of a sort, yet she could not regard the visit as a success. Lady Anne was no Society hostess. Lady Cowper might acknowledge them if they met by chance, but was unlikely to go out of her way to invite them. And though Meg had been the most successful at breaking barriers, even she now looked glum.

CHAPTER NINE

"IF ONLY WE HAD a respectable address!" Meg cried passionately from her usual hopeful post at the morning-room window. "They were friendly until Sir Gideon asked permission to call and they found out where I live."

"So you have told us a hundred times," said Thea without raising her eyes from her book. "Can you think of nothing else? At least stop talking about it, for Penny will be down soon."

"Do come and sit down, dear," their mother said in mild reproof, her fingers busy with a netting shuttle. "If anyone *should* call, they would be shocked to see you peering out at them like an ill-bred schoolgirl."

Thea set aside the book. "Shall I help you with that difficult bit of drawn-thread work you gave up on last night?"

Her volatile sister was happily absorbed in her needlework when Penny came in, pale after her daily bout of morning sickness.

"You all enjoy embroidery," she said, smiling, "yet I recall Meg telling me that none of you is a good needlewoman."

"That was when we had to do all the plain sewing," Meg explained. "Shifts and sheets and suchlike we managed, though they were so very dull! We are all utterly inept when it comes to making patterns for gowns and stitching them together so that they fit." She dropped her work, ran to Penny, and hugged her. "Dearest Penny, you are a darling to be so generous to us. It is fun sewing little, pretty things, but I vow I never want to make up a gown again. Now come and sit down by the fire and I shall bring your footstool."

Meg was fussing with shawls and fire-screens when a thunderous knocking at the front door startled them all. The bell pealed violently three times, then, in a sudden hush, they heard hurried footsteps in the hall as Dunmow rushed to answer the summons. Before he reached the door, the din resumed.

The thunder ended in a crash and a bellow. "Where's my niece?"

Penny turned deathly white. "Uncle Vaughn," she whispered.

Thea had almost forgotten about Mr. Vaughn since the evidence of his malice had been concealed by the redecorating. She knew he had driven Penny to elope with Dr. Angus Knox, but she knew little else, as Penny refused to talk about him.

"Y-your niece, sir?" stammered Dunmow in the hall.

"Lady Kilmore, she calls herself now, the ungrateful hussy."

"Her ladyship is not at home," the butler said resolutely. His dignity would be irreparably compromised if he admitted to the house someone who called his mistress a hussy.

The ladies listening petrified in the morning-room heard a thud and a gasp.

"Not at home? If you mean she's not receiving visitors, she'll see her uncle or I'll tear the place down about her ears."

"I believe her ladyship is still abovestairs." Dunmow sounded shaky.

"Then go and see, man!" roared the intruder.

The butler did his best to regain his composure. "Whom shall I announce, sir?"

"Say her dearest Uncle Vaughn has come to pay a bride visit." The suddenly smooth, unpleasant tone was somehow more frightening than his noisy threats.

"Jason!" Penny moaned faintly. "Oh, Jason, where are you?"

Meg, her eyes bright with excitement, patted her arm. The dowager cowered in her chair. Thea discovered her hands were trembling. Every gaze was fixed on the door to the hall in horrified anticipation.

Dunmow entered through the connecting door to the dining-room. "To mislead him as to your whereabouts, my lady," he explained in a hoarse whisper, exploring his shoulder gingerly with his other hand.

"That was clever of you," Thea said softly, though it could not delay the brute more than a few seconds. "Did he hit you?"

"Yes, miss, but it's all right." He straightened his back, tugged down his waistcoat, smoothed his black coat, and continued in a low voice, "Mr. Vaughn to pay a bride visit, my lady, and what are we to do? He's too big for me to tackle alone, and that's a fact."

"The footmen?" Thea asked, though she knew the answer all too well.

"George is out running errands, miss, and it's Geoffrey's day off."

"I'll tell him Penny is ill and cannot see him," Meg suggested with undaunted spirit.

She was so small and young and pretty, he would never take her seriously. If he came to blows again, she might be badly injured. Thea stood up, taking a deep breath.

"I shall speak to Mr. Vaughn, Dunmow," she said, amazed at the steadiness of her voice. "We shall go through the dining-room."

He followed her reluctantly, hanging back.

Mr. Vaughn was still in the hall, near the open front door, staring suspiciously at the morning-room door. A fleshy bear of a man, tall, with massive shoulders slightly hunched, clenched fists half raised, his very presence was a threat. His clothes, once good, were neat but on the verge of shabbiness, his boots well polished but run down at the heels.

"Mr. Vaughn?"

He swung round, glowering, reddish eyes overshadowed by a heavy brow. "Who're you?" A whiff of stale gin accompanied the words.

"Thea Kilmore, Penelope's sister-in-law." She held herself tightly, afraid that if she relaxed a single muscle she would turn and run. "She is unwell and cannot see anyone."

"Unwell, hey? Doing it too brown, missy. She's never ill."

"I assure you, sir, she is not fit to receive guests."

"Got a bun in the oven, I suppose. At it like rabbits, they was, before the ink hardly dried on their marriage lines. I'm no guest, though. Family, I am. Her own mother's brother-in-law. She'll see me, or she'll regret it."

I must keep him talking, Thea thought. Perhaps he would calm down. Perhaps George would return soon. "I will take her a message. What is your business with her?"

"Business! Two years of my life I gave the jade, neglecting my own business so as I could take care of her affairs for her, treating her like a daughter, and what do I get? She up and cheats me, runs off with that fine, featherless brother of yours, and not a shilling do I get for my trouble."

Thea's glance flew round the hall: the Turkey carpet, the cherrywood half-moon table, brocade-covered side chairs, gilt-framed mirror. She remembered the stark bareness that had met their arrival in Russell Square. *Not a shilling?* she almost asked aloud. "You need money?"

"I've got a good scheme on the cards." He was whining now. "All I need's a spot of the ready to invest. And her aunt's ill again. Doctors and medicines cost a mint."

"I am sorry, sir, but Penny does not handle her own finances." She tried to speak firmly. "You must consult my brother, and the lawyers."

"Bloody lawyers, is it?" he shouted. "And your bloody brother? I'll see 'em in Hell first. She'll shell out if I have to shake every penny out of her. And I don't take kindly to them as stands in my way." He advanced on her, his angry face suffused with blood, his fist raised.

Behind him in the doorway a tall figure appeared. In three strides Lord Hazlewood was between Thea and Mr. Vaughn, his back to her. Though of a height with the bully, his shoulders near as broad, he was far less massive.

Thea could not bear it if he were hurt. Hands clasped in a plea, she stepped forward as the two men stared at each other. Dunmow reached for her arm and tugged her back, shaking his head. He was watching them, his face intent but unworried.

Then she saw them as the butler did. The marquis was fit and trim where his adversary was flabby. Relaxed yet wary, Lord Hazlewood's stance contrasted with Vaughn's aggressive rigidity.

Penny's uncle was now livid with fury, whereas Lord Hazlewood's voice, at least, had lost none of its accustomed calm. "You are not welcome in this house, I think."

"What's it to you where I'm welcome?" snarled Vaughn.

"A lady's wishes must be the natural concern of any gentleman."

"To the devil with a lady's wishes! It's no lady I've come to see but my niece, and you've got no right to keep me from her." He rushed forward, fists flailing.

Thea gasped as the marquis stepped suddenly aside, his arms moving too quickly for her to follow. Vaughn staggered backwards, clutching his belly, his eyes dazed. Making an involuntary exit through the open front door, he lost his balance on the step and sat down, hard.

"If you'll pardon the liberty, my lord," said Dunmow admiringly, "you've a punishing left. I wager your lordship strips to advantage. Spar with the Gentleman, do you?"

"Jackson has honoured me with a few rounds." Lord Hazlewood's gaze never left his opponent. He strode forward to the threshold and looked down at him. "You will not come near this house again, nor attempt to speak to any of the ladies residing here." No longer merely cool, his voice was bitingly cold, with an undertone of controlled violence that suggested he was tempted to follow up his victory with a sound drubbing.

Instead, he stepped back and closed the door with such care that the latch barely clicked. He turned. "My dear girl!"

Thea found herself in his arms and realized she was shaking. She could not stop. She closed her eyes and pressed her forehead against his cravat.

"My dear girl," he said again, holding her tightly, "I'm sorry. I ought to have seen you out of the way first, though I somehow doubt the rogue would have waited. Still, a fine gentleman I've proven myself! No lady should be subjected to such a sight. It's all over now. He will not trouble you again. It's all right. It's all over."

His gentle strength encompassed her, soothed her. In a daze she clung to him. And then her mother was there, waving smelling salts. Meg chattered, explaining matters to the marquis and admiring Thea's bravery. They took her into the morning-room, sat her down by the fire opposite Penny, and chafed her icy hands.

Penny huddled in her chair, still stunned. It was to her Lord Hazlewood took the first glass of wine he poured when Dunmow brought in the decanters from the dining-room. He wrapped her fingers around the stem of the glass and, when she stared blankly at it, raised it to her lips. Sipping, she gradually recovered a little colour.

Dunmow brought Thea a glass. The Madeira warmed her inside, chasing away the last vestiges of shock.

"Feeling better?" The marquis, seated by Penny, smiled at Thea. "I must once again apologize for exposing you to fisticuffs, Miss Kilmore. Will would have my hide for behaving with such bad ton."

"You cannot think me so ungrateful as to complain when you have saved Penny from that dreadful man. How can we ever thank you?"

He looked disconcerted. "By not mentioning it again, if you please, and in particular by not revealing to my cousin my lapse from good taste."

Meg said mischievously, "I shall tell Mr. DeVine you illustrated splendidly his explanation of the difference between a sporting gentleman, who wagers on sports, and a sportsman, who participates."

"Good gad, don't tell me you were watching, too!"

"No, alas. Mama would not let me open the door until she was sure it was over."

The dowager, having slipped from the room unnoticed, now returned with salve and bandages. In her quiet way she insisted on examining the marquis's hands for bruises and abrasions. Though he let her spread salve on his knuckles, he refused bandages.

"I could not put on gloves over them, ma'am," he explained. "They would be noticed. The quieter we keep this business, the better for everyone, I believe." He threw a minatory glance at Meg.

"Surely you trust Mr. DeVine's discretion," she teased.

Her mother intervened in one of her infrequent exercises of authority. "You will tell no one, Meg dear. There is no need for Jason to know, since Lord Hazlewood has dealt with the man, and Penny cannot want it known that she has so... so *barbaric* a relative."

"Mr. Vaughn is no blood relation, Mama," Thea reminded her. She was worried about Penny's continuing muteness. "He married Penny's mama's sister."

"So he has no legal claim on Lady Kilmore whatever," said Lord Hazlewood in relief. "I am glad to hear it. Now, ladies, pray let us put the whole affair behind us. I am come to invite you *all* to dine in Arlington Street on Wednesday."

"THE KILMORES AGAIN!" hissed Lady Hazlewood. Her irritation got the better of her sense of propriety. "Are you enamoured of that woman? She is large enough for you, at all events."

"Lady Kilmore has an admirably statuesque figure," Rod agreed mildly, "and I have considerable respect for her, but no, I am in no way enamoured. Even in my salad days I never stole another man's wife."

"He would not stand in your way, I daresay. The on-dit is that he has already tired of the vulgar mushroom and spends all his time in the clubs."

Troubled, Rod was unable to refute the scandalmongers. He himself had seen Jason Kilmore at White's, Brooks's, and Boodle's, engaged in the admittedly innocuous occupation of talking to members. Still, it was none of his affair. "He will accompany the ladies on Wednesday," he said. He had made sure of that before setting the date.

"Wednesday! In my state of health, how do you expect me to arrange a dinner party at such short notice?"

"If my cook cannot provide a first-rate dinner with four days' notice, I shall dismiss him. If you are not well enough to produce a list of guests in an hour or so, I shall do so myself—and ask Aunt Anne to be my hostess."

His provocation succeeded. "You cannot be serious. Anne has no more notion of... I am perfectly capable of making up a list, Hazlewood, but if you wish to in-

vite more than four or five, I fear my hand is too weak
to write so many invitations so quickly.''

"I daresay my next speech in the House can wait long
enough for Johnson to send out a dozen invitations.''
In fact, his secretary almost invariably dealt with the
marchioness's correspondence as well as his own. The
poor relation hired to perform that office for her, ac-
cused of fretting her nerves to flinders, had been dismissed. No doubt she was much happier in her present
post as companion to his eldest sister.

John Johnson was another distant cousin in reduced
circumstances. A reserved, scholarly man a few years
older than Rod, he was not at all surprised when his
employer told him not to send out any invitations without his approval of the list. He took it up to the marquis's dressing-room shortly before dinner.

Neckcloth in hand, Rod scanned it. ''Oh lord, this
will never do,'' he groaned.

"Need a hand with your cravat?'' asked Will, ap-
pearing on the doorstep.

"Thank you, no. I prefer to be able to breathe. No,
it's this list Mother has made up for dinner on Wednesday.''

Will took it and perused it with growing indignation.
''I'll be damned if she hasn't invited all the dullest,
starchiest people in Town!''

"And those least likely to entertain the Kilmores later
on,'' said Rod grimly, winding snow-white muslin about
his neck and tying it in a neat, plain knot. ''I'll wear the
topaz pin, Pelham.''

"John, have you a pencil?'' Will demanded.
''Thanks. The Venables and the Fetherstonehaughs can
go for a start.'' He drew a firm line through their names.

"Yes, substitute the Duke and Duchess of Trent. He is a dolt and she has a malicious tongue, but she did at least speak to Lady Kilmore. Besides, they do entertain, and a duke always adds a certain cachet to an occasion."

"With luck she will keep my aunt happy, too. We'll have to do away with Lord Henry, even if he is her brother. He's a crashing bore. And the Drummond Burrells—far too high in the instep. Lord and Lady Cowper will be much better." He scribbled busily. "Good gad, the Trevelyans!"

"Mother must have thought including one of my political associates would make me overlook the rest," said Rod absently as his valet helped him don his coat. "She left Aunt Anne off, did she not? Write her in. Who were those people Miss Megan was talking to?"

"Giddy Turner, his mother and sister, and the Lewins." The pencil flew.

"That should do it. I don't want the Kilmores overwhelmed by a crowd."

Will gave the new list to the secretary, who rapidly read down it. "Too many females, sir," he said. "You will need another five gentlemen to balance the table."

"You shall attend, John," said Rod. "And we had really better put Uncle Henry back. Any friends of yours, Will?"

"Most of 'em are terrified of my aunt. I could probably talk Pretty Pritchard into it."

"That would be the Honourable Everett Pritchard?" asked Johnson warily.

"Right. He has lodgings at the Albany. Who else?"

"Add Lord Stewart," Rod instructed. "I met him at Brooks's the other day. He's out of mourning for his wife and he's an obliging fellow. Is that enough?"

"One more, sir."

"Uncle Reggie," Will proposed. "They know him. He'll make up for your Uncle Henry, coz, the one an unmitigated bore, the other guaranteed to liven things up."

"I'm not sure I want things quite *that* lively, but you're right, they are acquainted with him."

"That will be twenty-six altogether, a good number," said the secretary with satisfaction. "I'll send the invitations out tonight."

Twenty-six was considerably more than Rod had intended. He was afraid such a crowd would overawe Thea. But it was she who wanted her sister launched and her sister-in-law accepted in Society.

"Excellent," he said.

CHAPTER TEN

"THEA, DO YOU THINK the amber beads are dowdy?" Penny asked anxiously.

"Not at all. They are perfect with that russet silk."

"And modest enough not to offend? I do not want people to stare at me and think, 'Ah yes, the heiress.'"

"My dear, you are every inch a lady." Jason came into the dressing-room and dropped a light kiss on his wife's cheek. "Your gown is stylish, yet not so *dernier cri* as to arouse envy. The colour is perfect for you. You look very well tonight."

Thea thought she looked beautiful, and wished her brother had said so. Penny took his words differently.

"I *feel* well, Jason," she said, with a pleading glance that he did not notice as, at that moment, he turned to the mirror to straighten his neckcloth.

He was still sleeping in his dressing-room every night, Thea knew. In fact, *everyone* knew it. Her mother considered that he was showing a praiseworthy concern for Penny's delicate condition, so Thea kept to herself her own opinion that he was only making Penny miserable. But even if she had had more faith in her own perspicacity, she was quite unable to imagine herself telling her brother to sleep with his wife.

That worry faded when they reached the cul-de-sac at the end of Arlington Street and came to a halt behind a line of carriages turning into the Hazlewoods' court-yard. Meg peered out of the window.

"How splendid! There will be *dozens* of people at dinner," she said excitedly.

"Oh, no!" Thea was dismayed. "I expected a small party, little more than ourselves and the Hazlewood household."

Jason laughed. "Hardly! I imagine Hazlewood merely added us to an existing guest list, though he'd have to invite a few extra gentlemen as well. Don't worry, Thea." He reached across and patted her hand. "You can lose yourself in the crowd."

The carriage moved on, then jolted to a sudden stop. "Tha great gowk!" Scargill bawled from the box as some other coachman cut him off in the confusion. Fortunately, his North Country insult went unheeded. A moment later they pulled up before the magnificent portico, brightly lit by modern gas lamps.

George, in his blue-and-maroon livery, jumped down from the back. He rushed to vie with one of the Hazlewood footmen in opening the carriage door, letting down the step, and handing out the ladies.

Thea shivered as she stepped down. It was all very well Jason saying she could lose herself in the crowd, but at dinner she'd have to sit between two gentlemen, who would expect her to converse with them. As host, the marquis would take in the highest-ranking lady guest. As an unmarried lady of no importance, Thea could not expect to sit anywhere near him.

No doubt Will DeVine had arranged to partner Meg, while Jason and Penny, being comparatively newly wed, might well go in together. The best Thea dared hope for was to have either Will or Jason seated beside her. Her partner was sure to be a stranger.

The butler announced them, and they proceeded into the long drawing-room. Lord Hazlewood stepped forward to greet them, but his mother was there before him.

Gliding forward, the marchioness took the dowager's hand and cooed, "I am so happy you were able to come. My dear madam, let me make you acquainted with my guests. Lady Cowper, have you met Lady Kilmore? One of the dearest companions of my youth, you must know. We lost touch over the years and met again recently by the luckiest chance."

Utterly bewildered, the dowager stammered a few words to Lady Cowper, then her hostess swept her on towards the Duchess of Trent.

Emily Cowper, a twinkle in her grey eyes, said to Jason, "I met your wife the other day, Kilmore. You are a lucky man. Lady Kilmore, permit me to present my husband."

Will DeVine and Mr. Glubb-ffoulkes were bearing down on Meg, the former moving with deceptively casual swiftness, the latter making no effort to disguise his wheezing eagerness.

Amused, Lord Hazlewood said to Thea, "It was my cousin's notion to invite his uncle. I wager he had forgotten he has a rival there."

"I daresay he is confident of his superior attractions. Sir, I do not understand why Lady Hazlewood called my mother an old friend. Mama has the vaguest recollection of having once exchanged bows with her, but they were never on anything approaching intimate terms. And when we came before . . ." She hesitated.

"She scarcely treated Lady Kilmore as a long-lost bosom bow. I'd not say this to anyone else, but I suspect my mother is simply protecting her reputation."

"For exclusivity? Yes, of course. She would not want anyone to guess that you coerced her into entertaining a family she holds in contempt."

"Not contempt! You must believe Will when he says that she disapproves of half the ton."

"But you did coerce her, did you not, sir?"

He smiled down at her. "In the mildest fashion. I told her that if she did not care to act as my hostess for this dinner, I should invite Aunt Anne to do so. Ah, here are the Trevelyans. Come and meet them. Trevelyan and I worked together on a government select committee this past year."

Thea turned as the butler announced, "Mr. and Mrs. Trevelyan."

Mr. Trevelyan looked quite ordinary. His petite young wife reminded Thea of Meg. Though her eyes were a startling blue, her curls black rather than dark brown, she had the same lively, friendly air.

Her husband frowned when the marquis introduced Thea. Mrs. Trevelyan seemed somewhat startled but she said cordially, "I am happy to meet you, Miss Kilmore. Is your brother here?"

"Alison!" said Mr. Trevelyan on a warning note.

"Yes, Jason is here," said Thea, puzzled, "and my new sister-in-law."

"We saw the announcement of his marriage in the *Gazette,* did we not, Philip? I was so pleased. I should like to meet Lady Kilmore."

"Later, perhaps." Mr. Trevelyan took her arm in a firm clasp. "Pray excuse us, Miss Kilmore. We must speak to our hostess." They moved on.

The dawning dismay on Lord Hazlewood's face jogged Thea's memory. "Alison!" she whispered. "Oh, surely not!"

"I'm afraid so," he said grimly. "What a fool I am! I should have known Mother would not invite my friend only to be conciliating, but I have little patience with gossip and the connection momentarily slipped my mind."

"Then it *was* Mrs. Trevelyan Jason once attempted to abduct? And everyone knows? What will she do?"

"I cannot guess. Fortunately Trevelyan appears to be in command of himself and his wife and to have no particular desire to come to cuffs with your brother. But how do you know the tale? Surely he did not tell you?"

"No, he told Penny." Thea racked her brains to recall what Penny had said. "Of course, she was Alison Something Else then. With luck, Penny will not find out who Mrs. Trevelyan is."

"I sincerely hope not. I would not have had this happen for the world."

She laid her hand on his arm. "You must not think that I hold you accountable for...oh, dear!"

He grimaced. "For my mother's troublemaking? Thank you, my dear."

"Oh no, I am sure Lady Hazlewood cannot have realized how awkward the situation would be."

"You are generous." He would have said more, but Mr. Glubb-ffoulkes came creaking up to them.

"Delighted to discover I'm to take you in to dinner, Miss Kilmore," he puffed, beaming.

Mr. DeVine's uncle proved an undemanding dinner partner. Most of his attention was concentrated on the succession of superb dishes set before them, from which he helped both himself and Thea with a lavish hand. On the rare occasions when he opened his mouth other than to put food in it, he entertained her with descriptions of the marvels to be found on the Prince Regent's table.

"Carême's the most highly paid chef in history," he informed her, "and he's worth every farthing. Prinny bribed him away from that Frenchie, Tallyho."

Tallyho sounded like an extraordinary name for a Frenchman, but Thea did not venture to quibble. She watched Meg, opposite, laughing with Will, and wished she could see her mother and Penny, who were both on the same side of the long table.

Her other neighbour was a Lord Stewart, who introduced himself to her as they sat down. A gentleman in his early forties, he had a pleasant face strongly marked by signs of grief. He had brought in Lady Anne, and during the first course Thea heard him conversing gravely with the self-announced bluestocking on some medical topic.

He turned to her as the second course was carried in. "I understand your home is in the North, Miss Kilmore," he said, and with a few kindly questions soon had her chatting about Newkirk, and about country life in general. She carefully avoided the subject of vegetable gardening.

All in all, dinner was not half so frightening as she had expected.

When the ladies retired to the drawing-room, leaving the gentlemen to circulate the port and brandy, Thea went straight to Penny. So did Alison Trevelyan.

Seeing no polite alternative, Thea introduced them. "Penny, this is Mrs. Trevelyan. Ma'am, my sister-in-law, Lady Kilmore."

"I have been hoping to make your acquaintance, Lady Kilmore," said Mrs. Trevelyan, with a smile in which Thea could read nothing but friendly interest. "Your home is in Russell Square, I understand? I was

brought up just around the corner, in Great Ormond
Street.''

As they chatted about the neighbourhood, Thea began to relax. Penny was cheerful and looking well. If
Mrs. Trevelyan held any grudge against Jason for her
abduction, she gave no sign of it. Artlessly charming,
she was as different from the spoiled, feather-headed
Henrietta as one pretty, dainty young lady could possibly be from another. Thea had never understood why
her brother chose to elope with Henrietta, but she felt
he might well have been genuinely enamoured of the
present Mrs. Trevelyan.

"I shall be holding my first formal dinner party
soon,'' Mrs. Trevelyan confided. ''I do hope you will
come, Lady Kilmore, Miss Kilmore, and your mother
and sister, of course. I shall send you an invitation
without fail. Now excuse me, pray. I must speak to
Lady Cowper.'' She pattered off.

"I like her," said Penny. "And it is such a relief to
meet someone else who was not brought up among the
aristocracy. Meg will be pleased with the invitation. I
daresay she will receive others, for she appears to be on
excellent terms with those two girls over there.''

Thea glanced at her sister, who was giggling with a
pair of young ladies who looked familiar. "I believe
those are the two she met here before. How thoughtful
of Lord Hazlewood to invite them. And Mama is having a comfortable cose with Lady Anne. Oh Penny, the
Duchess of Trent is coming this way. I hope she does not
mean to join us.''

"Fustian! It will do our credit no end of good if her
grace chooses to speak to us. Good evening, ma'am.''

"Good evening, Lady Kilmore, Miss Kilmore.'' The
duchess, an imposing woman in black silk, swooped

down upon them like a crow on a cornfield. Her mocking smile was directed at Penny. "How wise of you to accept Mrs. Trevelyan's overtures," she said.

"I beg your pardon, ma'am? I fear I don't understand you."

Thea understood, all too well. Her grace must have guessed that Penny didn't know who Alison Trevelyan was. Bent upon mischief, she was about to enlighten her.

"Why, are you not aware that your husband once ran off with Mrs. Trevelyan? Alison Larkin, she was then. Of course, that was in his salad days, all of five months since."

Penny turned quite white, but she straightened her shoulders and raised her chin. "I hardly think, ma'am, that it is proper in any wife to enquire into her husband's wild oats. Unmarried gentlemen are traditionally granted a certain licence, are they not?"

"They are indeed," the duchess agreed with ironic approval. "And they say that reformed rakes make the best husbands. May I hope that you will call on me one day soon, Lady Kilmore? I am at home on Saturdays."

With a gracious nod, she left them. Before Thea could do more than take Penny's hand, Lady Cowper was upon them.

"The Duchess of Trent is a malicious tattlemonger," she said forthrightly. "Alison Trevelyan is a kind-hearted child, and you, Lady Kilmore, are a sensible woman. If you will permit me to advise you, you cannot do better than to follow Mrs. Trevelyan's lead."

"Yes, ma'am," Penny whispered, clutching Thea's hand.

"She tells me she has invited you to dinner. You must accept. The more cordial that relations between you are seen to be, the less food for gossip."

"Yes, ma'am."

"There is no denying Kilmore was something of a scapegrace, but play your part well and you will be the making of him. I shall leave my card in Russell Square. Come now, both of you, and let me present you to Lady Lewin and Lady Turner. Your sister—Miss Megan, is it not?—seems to be getting along splendidly with their daughters."

The good-natured countess led them across the room. Introduced by one of Almack's patronesses, they were naturally received with complaisance if not warmth. Lady Turner went so far as to say Meg was a pretty-behaved child, and Lady Lewin complimented Penny on her gown. The talk turned to modistes. To spare Penny, Thea racked her brains for something to say, but Penny, though still pale, was equal to the challenge of polite conversation.

All Thea had to do was listen and wonder how three grown women could talk so much without saying anything of significance. She didn't think she would ever learn the knack.

The ladies both admitted to spending most of their time in the country with their young families, and neither seemed to have heard about Jason and Alison Trevelyan. Lady Cowper was right, Thea thought. If Penny and Mrs. Trevelyan appeared to be friends, new talk of the abduction would soon die for want of fuel—as long as Jason cooperated.

She watched for him when the gentlemen came in. The first to arrive were Will DeVine, Lady Turner's son, and another young man, dressed with neat propriety.

All three made a beeline for Meg and her new friends, and Mr. Glubb-ffoulkes creaked along not far behind.

Jason and an older gentleman entered together, deep in conversation. They paused just inside the door and shook hands, then Jason looked around the room. As he made straight for Penny, the man he had been talking to followed at his heels. He turned out to be Lord Lewin.

After a brief confusion of introductions, Jason turned to Penny and said quietly, "I think you are tired, my dear. Do you wish to go home?"

She bit her lip. "We cannot drag Meg away when she is enjoying herself so."

"I can very well take you and return for the others."

"Oh. I am a little tired. Perhaps it would be best but..."

Thea nudged her and nodded towards Lady Hazlewood. The marchioness was watching with a smug air. She had most certainly invited the Trevelyans for the express purpose of discomfitting Penny, and she thought she had succeeded in ridding herself of the Cit's daughter.

Penny stiffened. "Thank you, Jason, but I should like to stay. I should hate to appear discourteous or ungracious when Lord Hazlewood went to so much trouble to arrange an agreeable party."

Jason looked daggers at the marquis, who had just joined them.

"I am glad you have met agreeable people under my roof, Lady Kilmore," he said, "but I must share the credit for choosing our guests with my mother."

"Ah," Jason murmured, enlightened. He and Lord Hazlewood exchanged a glance of mutual comprehension. "No doubt the marchioness has her own notions as to what constitutes an agreeable party."

Thea was relieved that the two men had reached an understanding, but she blenched as she saw Alison Trevelyan approaching, tugging her husband in her wake. Mr. Trevelyan's expression was determinedly blank.

Before they arrived, Lord Stewart came up to her and launched into an amusing story about his younger son's prowess on his new pony. Her attention divided, Thea hoped her comments were appropriate. She caught only enough of the nearby conversation to gather that Jason and Mr. Trevelyan were discussing the weather with stiff politeness. Penny and Mrs. Trevelyan had their heads, one black, one flaming red, together in apparent intimacy, slightly fixed smiles on both their faces.

"Do you ride, Miss Kilmore?" Lord Stewart asked.

"I? Ride? Yes, sir. That is, I used to, some years ago."

"You do not care for the exercise?"

"I was used to enjoy it greatly. One can see so much more of the countryside than on foot."

"I have a quiet mare. May I hope that you will ride with me in the Park one fine day? It cannot compare with your moors, alas."

"Hyde Park? With you?" Thea asked in astonishment. Taken aback, he blinked at her and she added hastily, "I should be delighted, my lord, but I have no habit."

"Then perhaps you will not be averse to driving in my phaeton, ma'am? Tomorrow afternoon, if you have no other engagements?" He took silence for consent. "I shall call for you at three, if that suits?"

"Th-thank you, sir." In a daze, she gave her direction. "We reside in Russell Square."

Once more taken aback, Lord Stewart rallied gallantly. "Three o'clock tomorrow, then. Excellent. Ah, the tea tray is come, I see. Allow me to bring you a cup."

He was too late. Disconsolate, he went to fetch his own as Lord Hazlewood appeared at Thea's elbow bearing two steaming cups.

"We have brushed through the worst," he said in a low voice. "Lady Kilmore and Mrs. Trevelyan have my utmost respect."

"Yes, they were splendid," she said vaguely, still feeling stunned. "Sir, Lord Stewart is taking me for a drive in Hyde Park tomorrow."

"Stewart!" He frowned.

"Is that not proper? Oh dear, when he asked me I was so surprised I forgot that he is married."

"Widowed, so it will be perfectly proper," he conceded with reluctance. "You have your mother's consent?"

"I don't believe she has met him, but I am sure neither you nor Lady Hazlewood would invite a gentleman of whom she might disapprove. Besides, I am by far too old to run to Mama for permission."

"For permission, yes, but I hope in future you will consult her before you accept invitations."

"I will, I promise. Only, Mama is not well acquainted with the ton. She would not know that Lord Stewart is a widower."

"True. You had best ask me—or your brother. If Stewart had in fact still been a married man, you might have placed yourself in an awkward position."

Thea's growing confidence crumbled. She had begun to think that entering Society might not be so daunting after all, and now she realized there was many a pitfall awaiting her.

Her only consolation was that Lord Hazlewood had offered to advise her, which suggested he meant to be available to be asked.

CHAPTER ELEVEN

"HE WANTED to leave me at home," wept Penny, hunched on the edge of Thea's bed, "and go back without me."

"He was worried about your health," Thea insisted. "You cannot suppose that he hoped to be able to speak privately with Mrs. Trevelyan, with her husband there, and everyone else. I cannot believe he is still interested in her, now that she is married."

"Perhaps not, but did you notice how like Henrietta she is?"

"Like Henrietta? Heavens, no. She seemed to me to be quite like Meg, though I did not see enough of her to be certain to what extent their characters are similar."

"Similar in character, perhaps, and she and Meg are both dark, whereas Henrietta is blond. Either is more fashionable than red hair!"

"Your hair is beautiful, Penny."

"Most people think it freakish. No, I meant all three are small and delicate. Jason is attracted to small, delicate females and I am tall and... and *solid*." She clasped her arms about her middle, which as yet showed no signs of thickening. "And I shall soon be solider than ever."

Thea's face grew hot as she pointed out, "You would not be pregnant if he were not attracted to you."

"Doubtless he wants an heir," Penny said bitterly. "If I do not provide one this time, he will return to my bed. In the meantime, he is never at home and he sleeps in his dressing-room. I cannot even tell whether he has spent the night at home. I am sure he has taken a mistress."

"Oh Penny, no! How can you say such a thing?"

"Lots of married men do. I suppose every wife hopes her husband will be different." Tears streaked down her cheeks. "I love him, Thea. I want him so. The only thing I can think of is to go on a reducing diet and hope that if I am thin enough he will come back to me."

"Is that wise when you are increasing? You should be eating for two. You must ask Mama."

"I cannot! She seems to think I should be glad that Jason does not 'bother' me."

"I daresay that is because she was always happier when my father was away, which indeed was most of the time."

"She does not understand. She will not understand why I want to lose weight. Promise you will not tell her," Penny begged. "How can eating just a little less hurt the baby when it is still no bigger than the tip of my thumb?"

"I don't know." Thea wished she had taken more interest in medical matters.

"Promise?"

"I promise," she said unwillingly, "but you must promise to eat more if you feel at all ill."

Penny grimaced. "I feel ill enough every morning without making it worse on purpose. Perhaps I shall feel better. Oh, look, it is ten to three and we have not settled what you are to wear to drive out with your admirer. Quick, ring for Farden while I wash my face."

She dashed to the washstand and splashed her eyes with a little cold water from the forget-me-not-painted ewer.

Tugging the bell-pull, Thea protested, "Lord Stewart is not an admirer. He is a widower with dozens of children."

"Dozens?"

"Lots, anyway. I could not keep count. All he wants is a sympathetic ear to listen to his stories about them. As long as he expects nothing from me but murmurs of admiration, I shall be safe." She returned to the subject of clothes as the abigail came in. "Shall I wear the periwinkle blue pelisse? I have no time now to change my dress and it will hide this one."

"That will do very well, with the bonnet trimmed with periwinkles, Farden," Penny directed. "We must go tomorrow to order a riding habit for you, Thea. Chocolate brown, with apricot braiding, and a small, brown cork hat with just one apricot feather curling around it. You will look excessively dashing."

"Dashing?" Thea laughed. "I shall give quite the wrong impression then, for no one could be less dashing. Besides, I doubt I shall need it. I have not been on a horse this age and I fear I should make a cake of myself before half the ton."

Meg put her head around the door, then came in. "Are you ready to go down, Thea? After what Lord Hazlewood said, I am determined not to be one of those ladies who keeps gentlemen waiting."

"How pretty you look, Meg. That shade of peach is perfect for you. I daresay you would be forgiven if you were late. Which of your beaux is driving you, did you say?"

"Sir Gideon, in his curricle, but Mr. DeVine and Mr. Pritchard mean to ride alongside," said Meg blithely.

"Did I tell you what they call each other? Giddy, of course, and Pretty, and the Divine Will! Is that not shocking?" She giggled. "Do come on, Thea."

Penny followed them from Thea's chamber and stood at the top of the stairs, watching forlornly as they started down.

"You will come down, will you not?" Thea asked her.

"Oh, you need me as chaperon, of course. I forgot your mama has gone to visit Lady Anne."

"I am chaperon enough for Meg, but I should be glad of your support." Suddenly she panicked. "What am I to say to him, Penny? Suppose he does not want to talk about his children?"

Taking her arm, Penny urged her down the stairs. "It is for the gentleman to find a subject that the lady is comfortable discussing," she said. "If worst comes to worst, there is always the weather."

Thea was not forced to fall back upon the weather, as Lord Stewart had an ample fund of anecdotes about his family. In Hyde Park, leaves gilded by the pale autumn sunshine drifted down from the stately elms to land in barouches, landaus, phaetons and curricles. The ton was taking advantage of the fine afternoon to see and be seen. To Thea, Rotten Row seemed crowded, with strollers and riders as well as vehicles. She could not imagine how it must be during the Season.

Lady Lewin bowed to her from an elegant green barouche, and Miss Lewin waved. An unknown gentleman seated opposite them turned his head and raised his hat politely. Several times Lord Stewart greeted acquaintances or halted the phaeton to exchange a few words with friends. Each time he introduced Thea, but they did not stay long enough to tax her conversational powers.

Now and then she caught sight of Meg, bowling along in Sir Gideon's curricle with her mounted escort. They stopped to talk to a tall figure on a huge black horse. From a distance Thea recognized Lord Hazlewood.

At once Penny's woes returned to the forefront of her mind. The marquis would know what to do, how to find out, without actually asking Jason, whether he was unfaithful to his wife.

As Lord Stewart's phaeton approached the group, Lord Hazlewood bowed to Meg and rode on to meet it. Thea realized that in her escort's presence she could hardly ask the marquis for a private meeting.

Ahead of him, coming their way, was a smart grey whiskey picked out in scarlet. The reins of the high-stepping grey gelding were in the hands of a lady a few years older than Thea. She was wearing a scarlet outfit that emphasized her curvaceous figure, and as she approached the phaeton, she raised her whip in greeting.

"Lord Stewart, well met."

The carriages stopped side by side. The viscount introduced Thea to Mrs. Wilmington, who gave her a dismissive glance and turned the full force of sparkling blue eyes on Lord Stewart. Thea hardly noticed that she was cut out of their conversation, and she certainly did not care. Lord Hazlewood was riding up on her side of the phaeton.

Rod noted with some annoyance that Lord Stewart's attention was absorbed by Alicia Wilmington. Not that he blamed the fellow—the dashing widow held him captive with every coquettish trick at her command. Nor did Miss Kilmore appear to mind, so he ignored them.

"Are you enjoying yourself?" he asked her, smiling.

"Oh yes. The Park is very pleasant and I love the autumn colours of the trees. One thing our moors lack is tall trees, except in the most sheltered valleys."

"You would like Hazlemere, my Buckinghamshire place. The beech woods are beautiful at any season."

From the corner of his eye, he noted Mrs. Wilmington's quandary. He was a marquis, and even richer than Stewart, but he had skilfully avoided parson's mousetrap for many a year, whereas the viscount might well be in the market for a new wife.

She was unable to resist the challenge. "Good day, Lord Hazlewood," she broke in, flirting at him with long eyelashes.

Startled, Lord Stewart swung round. He had the grace to look abashed at the realization that he had been neglecting Miss Kilmore. Rod wished them both good-day and turned back to Thea, but the widow was not finished yet.

"I shall never forget those house parties at Hazlemere," she said with a languishing air.

"I am sorry that my presence has awakened sad memories of your late husband. We had best avoid each other in future, ma'am." Her pout almost made him grin. "Incidentally, Miss Kilmore, I received word this morning of your young protégée at Hazlemere."

"Rosie? How is she?" Thea asked eagerly.

"Flourishing, and learning her letters. Her brother is becoming an excellent tiger, as you will see if you will entrust yourself to my driving tomorrow—no, wait, I must be in the House—the day after. We might go to admire the trees in St. James's Park. There are very fine avenues in The Mall and Birdcage Walk."

"I should like it of all things," she assured him, more relieved than delighted, he noted.

Which of her dratted relatives needed his assistance now? he wondered resignedly.

Mrs. Wilmington had failed to recapture Stewart's entire attention. He made polite noises about not keeping her horse standing in the cold, although the sun was amazingly warm for late October.

"So thoughtful," she murmured, directing at him a dazzling smile that carefully excluded Rod and Thea. "Happy to make your acquaintance, Miss Kilmore." She drove on.

"I shall see you on Saturday, Miss Kilmore," Rod said as Stewart picked up his reins and the phaeton started off in the opposite direction.

Rather than appear to follow Mrs. Wilmington, Rod stopped to talk to Lady Fetherstonehaugh, though normally he would have passed his mother's crony with no more than a polite bow.

That reminded him of the marchioness's perfidy. Riding on towards Arlington Street, he decided it must be young Lady Kilmore for whom Thea wished to solicit his help. Meg was rapidly finding her own feet in Society; the vague, shy dowager had struck up an unlikely friendship with Aunt Anne; Kilmore could surely take care of himself.

Damn the man for his rakish past! Nonetheless, Rod felt himself responsible for the unfortunate meeting between Lady Kilmore and the Trevelyans. Although all had gone better than he had dared hope, Thea probably wanted his advice as to her sister-in-law's best course of action. Her faith in him was flattering, but he wished just once she would see him as something other than a white knight.

He sighed. Will would say it was his own fault, and the devil of it was, Will was quite likely right.

Dismounting in the stables, he handed Achilles's reins to his new tiger. The boy was too young and unsure of himself to be sent so far as Hampstead, he decided, but Billy was looking on jealously. Though the lad had chosen to pursue the career of footman, he was often to be found hanging around the stables.

"I just come down to order her la'ship's carridge, m'lord," he now said defensively, feeling his master's eyes upon him.

"You can take a message to Hampstead for me."

He brightened. "*Yes,* m'lord. To Mrs. Bradshaw?"

"Tell Mrs. Bradshaw I shall do myself the honour of dining with her this evening."

Sue's soothing presence was what he needed. He usually spent three or four nights a week in Hampstead, but somehow, since his return from Yorkshire, he had seen her only twice. He felt a twinge of guilt. He always let her know in advance if he intended to join her for dinner or if he was going to arrive after eleven o'clock; otherwise, when he was in Town, he expected her to be waiting for him. How many lonely evenings she had spent waiting in vain!

Later, on his way, he stopped at a jeweller's in Piccadilly and bought her a necklace of gold filigree set with pearls. She never asked him for precious gifts, as he knew other men's mistresses did. In fact, she rarely wore those he gave her, but she would have a nest egg to fall back on when their association ended.

His start of surprise made Achilles toss his head in confusion. *When their association ended?* Rod had never before envisaged an end to the comfortable relationship. Now what the devil had put that notion into his head?

He lost his train of thought as a barking dog dashed into the road and nipped at Achilles's heels. Already disconcerted, the gelding reared. Keeping his seat with difficulty, Rod calmed his mount, but the animal continued skittish all the way to Hampstead.

As always, a lamp burned in the front bow window of Sue's little house. Rod knocked on the door, then used his own key to let himself in. Emerging from the parlour, Sue caught him sniffing the savoury smell of frying onions.

"I'm ravenous!"

"Liver and bacon, with onions, as you can tell. A plebeian dish, I'm afraid, but the liver would not keep. Enid has made a fricassee of chicken as well, and a sweet omelette, but I could not find any good fish."

"My dear, a feast fit for a king. I shall do it justice." He kissed her cheek, then took off his coat and hung it on a peg behind the door, taking the jeweller's box from the pocket. He put it in her hands.

Her eyes flew to his face, with an almost fearful expression. "Roderick . . . is this goodbye?"

"No, no. Why should you think that? It just seemed to me a long time since I gave you anything pretty." With another twinge of guilt, he put his arm about her waist, not as slim as it used to be but a cosy armful. "Come into the parlour and open it."

Reassured, she exclaimed in delight over the delicate tracery of gold, the lustrous perfection of the pearls. He unfastened the plain gold chain she was wearing and put on the new necklace in its place. The creamy white skin above her low-cut silk bodice lent the pearls a richer sheen, and the gleam of gold drew answering highlights from her dark gold hair. She was as lovely, as desirable as ever. Why had the notion of leaving her ever crossed his mind?

Her maid announced dinner and they moved into the tiny, intimate dining-room.

While they ate, they chatted about a book Sue was reading, an amusing novel he had bought her by the author of *Pride and Prejudice*. The heroine of *Emma* aspired to rule the lives of all those about her, for their own good. In her own way, and with the best intentions, Emma stirred up as much distress as did Rod's mother.

"You are troubled," said Sue as they returned to the parlour. She poured him a glass of brandy and herself a cup of tea. "Do you wish to talk about what is amiss?"

Taking a chair opposite hers at the fireside, he told her how the marchioness had invited the Trevelyans deliberately to discomfit the Kilmores. He would not have dreamt of criticizing his mother to anyone but Will—and Thea, he realized.

In inviting Thea to be frank with him, he had had no intention of reciprocating with equal frankness. A quagmire spread before him. If he did not tread with care, he might find himself initiating all sorts of topics that ought not to be discussed with a young lady of gentle birth. He had taken upon himself to guide her, not to lead her astray.

Sue recalled him to the subject of his mother's mischief. "You blame yourself for not preventing Lady Hazlewood's scheme. You must not. It was simply an oversight."

"As head of the family, I must hold myself responsible for the behaviour of family members. I have not the excuse of fearing her ill health, since I know it to be imaginary."

"You cannot be responsible for her every little action. Rod, must she live with you? You said she has a generous jointure. Can she not set up her own household, with your help if necessary?"

"It would present a very odd appearance, when I have a large house in Town and a vast mansion at Hazlemere. Unless I take a wife."

"No!" Her soft cry of protest startled him. She busied herself refilling his glass and her own cup as she continued with forced calm, "You would be no more comfortable in a marriage of convenience than you are at present, perhaps less. I don't believe you can be satisfied with anything but mutual love."

"And I have no... *little* expectation of finding love after so many years without success, so I must find my comfort where I may. Come here, Sue."

CHAPTER TWELVE

IN THE MORNING, buffeted by a blustery, invigorating west wind, Rod took Achilles for a gallop across Hampstead Heath. By the time he turned homeward, a ragged pall of clouds hung threateningly over the city.

Not a good day to take a young lady driving in an open vehicle. The rain might hold off, but the boisterous wind would rock the light curricle dangerously. He dared not risk overturning. If, as he suspected, Thea urgently wanted a private word with him, she must contrive the opportunity.

He ordered out the Town carriage to carry him to Russell Square that afternoon. When it rolled up to the front door, he was amused to see the jubilant expression of his new under-footman, hanging on behind. For once Billy had triumphed over the ragamuffin who had usurped his seat in the curricle. Whether he would soon enough attain the impassivity proper to a footman was questionable, however. Rod was prepared to give him his chance, but if the marchioness caught him grinning like that, he'd be back in the stables in no time.

On the other hand, Lady Hazlewood's presence was scarcely conducive to grinning, so perhaps the lad was safe.

And that was exactly the sort of thing Rod might let slip to Thea, giving her a very odd notion of his loyalty to his family. He *must* take care what he said to her.

The Kilmores' butler admitted him to the house just as she came down the stairs, wearing a walking dress of straw-coloured merino. In one hand she carried a muff, and over her arm a dark brown cloak.

"I see that you, Miss Kilmore, like your sister, mean to deprive us gentlemen of all cause for complaint about dilatory females," he quizzed her.

Her all-too-rare smile revealed an unexpected, hitherto-unnoticed dimple. "I cannot let my little sister outdo me in politeness," she said, descending the last few stairs.

"Unfortunately, your efforts are for nothing. The weather is too inclement to drive in the curricle, I fear."

"Oh no!" Her face fell. "But it is not raining. I looked out just a moment ago."

"The wind is blowing in gusts strong enough to overset a light carriage, even with my weight as ballast. I cannot expose you to the danger."

"Then can we not walk in the park?"

"My dear girl, you would be blown to pieces."

"I do not mind if you do not. I loved to walk on the moors on just such a day as this, and I do miss the exercise. Besides, Mama and Penny and Meg have gone to call on Lady Cowper, who left her card yesterday as she promised, and some others. I ought not to entertain you here alone, ought I?" she asked uncertainly.

"No, nor to ride alone with me in a closed carriage." He wondered what was so desperate that she would brave the elements to talk with him. "If you truly wish to go to St. James's Park, you must bring your maid."

The abigail was appalled when the carriage stopped at the end of The Mall and Billy, holding onto his hat, came to open the door and let down the step.

"You'll never walk in this wind, miss!" cried the maid. "It'll blow you off your feet."

"I am not so feeble," Thea retorted. "If you do not care to come, Farden, you may wait in the carriage. Lord Hazlewood's footman will go with us."

"That I will, miss," said Billy, "but if y'lordship pleases, I'll leave me 'at be'ind."

Stepping out into the blast, Rod grabbed his beaver as it lifted from his head. "You may, Billy. Miss Kilmore, will you object if I do likewise?"

"Not at all," she said, tightening the drawstrings of her cloak's hood. He handed her down and told the coachman to follow them.

Leaves swirled about them as they set out down the avenue. Thea walked with a countrywoman's swinging stride, heading determinedly into the wind. Despite the drawstrings, her hood soon blew back and she raised a laughing, pink-cheeked, pink-nosed face to Rod.

"I shall not try to keep my hood up, since no one is here to see." Her brown eyes sparkled. "Is it not exhilarating? May we walk across the grass to the lake?"

"By all means." His delight matched her own. He could never have imagined that behind her timid façade dwelt this vital, free-spirited creature who revelled in battling the elements. She belonged in the country, wandering across the moors she loved, through fields and woods, or tending her vegetable garden. Only her devotion to her family could have dragged her to an alien world of drawing rooms and scandalmongers.

They reached the lake and strolled along the bank. Most of the ducks, swans and pelicans had deserted the ruffled water to roost under the trees. A bare willow thrashed its drooping branches and the ground was littered with twigs.

Thea was pensive now. Rod was not surprised when she glanced back to ensure that his footman was out of earshot, then turned to him and said, "I need your advice."

"I thought so. What is it?"

"It's Penny." She hesitated, the colour in her cheeks heightened. Her eyes cast down, she took a deep breath before blurting out, "She is afraid that Jason is unfaithful, and I cannot reassure her because I do not know. Do you think it is just a fancy due to her condition?"

Rod fought to hide his consternation. "My dear Miss Kilmore, how can I possibly say?"

"Gentlemen do take mistresses," she persisted.

It was his turn to colour, glad that she was not looking at him. "They do."

"Even married gentlemen. I . . . I think Papa probably did."

"Even married gentlemen. It does not necessarily indicate any lessening of regard for the wife."

"Oh, fustian! Penny loves him, and she is very unhappy." She stopped, took his arm, and gazed up at him with pleading eyes. "Can you . . . could you possibly find out if Jason has a mistress?"

"Good God, no!" His explosive response made her take a step backwards. He reached out to take her hands. "I beg your pardon for startling you, but it is quite impossible. For one gentleman to spy on another is out of the question."

Stubborn despite her alarm at his vehemence, she asked, "Could you not lead the conversation round to . . . to that subject? And see what he said?"

"No. Even if I were on sufficiently intimate terms with your brother. Though admittedly there are many men tasteless enough to gossip about their *chères amies,* I am not one of them."

"Then you have...?" She pulled her hands from his and clapped them to her mouth, her face crimson now. "Oh, I did not mean to pry. It is none of my business."

He closed his eyes, appalled at where mutual frankness had led him, just as he had feared. Who was he to hold himself superior to those of his indiscreet fellows who boasted or complained of their ladybirds?

"You are angry," she said timidly. "I'm sorry."

He was about to lose her trust, and that he could not endure. "Not angry with you," he said with a rueful smile. "It was my fault entirely. My tongue ran away with me."

"As did mine with me." Her smile was shy, but not fearful—thank heaven!

A yellow maple leaf was caught in her dark hair, and one braid, lashed by the wind, was escaping its pins. Rod did not dare offer to pin it up because what he really wanted to do was loosen its strands and bury his face in the soft silkiness. He was disgusted with himself. So this was what came of discussing lightskirts with a respectable young lady!

Plucking the leaf from her hair with unnecessary concentration, he said severely, "You would not speak so freely to anyone else, would you?"

She shook her head, eyes wide. "Of course not, Lord Hazlewood."

Her use of his title struck him as extraordinarily funny. "Good heavens," he exclaimed, "after such a conversation as we have had, surely you can bring yourself to address me as Roderick—when none are by, of course."

"If you will call me Thea."

"I will." He realized she was shivering. "Come, Thea, you are cold from standing. Do you wish to return to the carriage or walk on?"

She chose to walk on. The vigorous pace she set soon returned the roses to her cheeks. They circled the lake, talking of trees and the distinctive countryside of different parts of England.

Later, when Rod changed for dinner, Pelham produced a yellow maple leaf from his greatcoat pocket. "Tricky, that wind," the valet observed.

ENTERING THE HOUSE, Thea threw back her hood. Dunmow's startled gasp, quickly stifled, sent her to the hallway mirror. How dreadful that Roderick had seen her looking as if she had been dragged backwards through a haystack!

Not that he had seemed to mind. In fact for a moment she had thought he was going to...but of course that was wishful thinking—or rather, sheer imagination. He had probably been wondering whether to suggest that she pin up her hair.

She hurried upstairs, a horrified Farden at her heels.

"Didn't I tell you, miss, you'd get proper tousled in that wind? What his lordship must think!"

"It is much too late to worry about his lordship. Just help me tidy my hair before Mama comes home."

She had just settled in the drawing-room with a book when the others returned and joined her. Meg was *aux anges*.

"Everyone was so very amiable, Thea. You should have come with us. Lady Cowper welcomed us most kindly and introduced us to several people. I do believe we shall have vouchers for Almack's in the spring."

"Do not set your sights too high, my love," warned her mother. "Recall that any one of the patronesses can deny them."

"Why should they? Anyway, we shall have plenty of other entertainments. Thea, Lady Turner has invited us to an informal dance next week."

"Sir Gideon's doing," said Penny drily. "I suspect he is well nicknamed 'Giddy,' for he is wildly enamoured of Meg after only two or three meetings."

"He does cast sheep's eyes and sigh a great deal." Meg laughed. "But Maria—his sister—says he is forever falling in love, so I shall not take him seriously. Jane Lewin was at Maria's house, Thea, and she says her mama will ask us to her musicale. And the Duchess of Trent invited us to a card party." She wrinkled her nose. "It sounds horridly dull."

Thea turned to Penny in surprise. "You called on the duchess?"

"She asked me to, remember? One does not lightly ignore the request of a duchess, nor refuse an invitation."

"I only wish we could," said the dowager unhappily. "She makes me uneasy, and I do not know how to play at cards."

"Not at all?" Penny asked. "Thea? Meg? None of you play? Heavens, I shall have to teach you. Loo will be best. It is simple and usually played for low stakes."

"You mean we shall be expected to gamble?" cried Meg. "Oh, Penny, I had much rather not waste my pin-money when there are so many more interesting ways to spend it."

"I shall see that you have enough to play a few hands at silver loo. We need not stay long."

"Penny, are you well enough to attend all those parties?" Thea asked anxiously.

"I usually feel quite well in the evenings and...and perhaps Jason will go with us. Sometimes, at least. If I am not well, I shall send my excuses. I daresay I should not dance."

"Dance!" said Meg in a hollow voice. "I have just realized, Thea and I don't know *how* to dance. That is *much* worse than not playing cards."

"And as easily remedied," Penny said, "though I hope you will both learn quickly, since Lady Turner's hop is next week already. I shall hire a dancing master at once. I cannot promise to turn you into performers upon the harp or pianoforte before Lady Lewin's musicale, however!"

"No, Thea and I never learned, having no instrument, but if we are asked, we could sing one of our duets," Meg proposed.

"In public?" The very thought made Thea shudder. "Not I. Nor is there any need for me to learn to dance. This is Meg's come-out, not mine."

"Will you not?" said Penny, disappointed. "I did so want you as well as Meg to have fun in London, Thea."

"Of course you must," Meg insisted. "Pretty and elegant as you are, gentlemen are bound to ask you to dance. You cannot be forever telling them that you are too old, as if you were in your dotage."

Giving in, Thea agreed to join the lessons. In truth, she would be sorry to have to tell Lord Hazlewood she did not dance—if he should happen to ask her to stand up with him. Satisfied, Penny went off to rest before dinner, and Meg to look through her wardrobe and decide what to wear for the coming parties.

The dowager sighed. "It is very kind in Penny to give Meg her Season, and naturally it is what one must desire for a daughter, but I wish I did not have to attend soirées and balls. When I made my own début, I disliked mingling with crowds of strangers. Indeed, I was glad to marry your father, Thea, just to escape. I hoped that at my age I should not mind any longer, but I still shrink from facing all those people."

Though Thea was disconcerted to find herself her mother's confidante as well as Penny's, she understood all too well the dread of entering a crowded room. It wasn't fair that after the long, patient years of bringing up her daughters without help, Mama should have to suffer more for their sakes.

"Need you, Mama? I can very well take Meg to parties. You know I do not care to dance."

"My love, as an unmarried lady you are by no means old enough to chaperon Meg to parties, even if you return to your caps." The dowager had never quite approved when Penny persuaded Thea to give up that badge of the old maid.

"Penny is married," Thea pointed out.

"But Penny is only twenty-one."

"Between the two of us we combine matrimony and sufficient years. You need only go when Penny does not."

Her mother's relief was so gratifying that for a moment Thea almost forgot her own qualms.

CHAPTER THIRTEEN

"I TOLD YOU SO," Meg hissed as she and Thea waited behind Jason and Penny to reach their hostess. "Lady Turner is only calling it an informal hop because Maria has not been presented yet. It is a proper ball. Are you not glad you are wearing your best gown?" She glanced down complacently at her own dress, of white lace opening over a white sarcenet slip garnished with pink silk roses to match the rosebuds in her hair.

Thea had let Penny persuade her to make a change from her favourite blue. Her gown was yellow, a soft shade deeper than jonquil, less bright than canary. She knew it suited her, but dismay at the crush in the confined entrance hall overwhelmed her pleasure. Bejewelled matrons bemoaned the horrid squeeze; girls in white or pastels whispered and giggled; soberly clad gentlemen begged each other's pardon as they tried to protect their ladies' gowns from the crowd.

Fixing her gaze on Penny's moss green satin, Thea managed another step forward. "Half the ton must be here," she murmured.

Meg shook her head. "Heavens, no. It is quite a small house, hired for the Season. They have no garden at all. The ballroom is as large as the rest of the house put together, but I cannot imagine where they will put everyone. Maria said they invited two hundred people."

'Two hundred! How was Lord Hazlewood ever to find her among so many? Though he had already requested a dance, she would never be bold enough to seek him out. However, tall as he was, he would be easily found by those hopeful ladies daring enough to pursue him. In fact, she saw him now, as they turned a corner and reached the open doors of the ballroom. He was standing just beyond the group clustered about the receiving line, his fair head bent to listen to his companion.

The crowd parted for a moment and Thea recognized the beautiful Lady Daphne, her hand on the marquis's arm. Shaken by an emotion she refused to acknowledge, Thea turned her head away. She had no right to be jealous.

Had jealousy been possible, she would have found much cause for suffering it that evening. Lord Hazlewood was too great a matrimonial prize for his long and resolute bachelorhood to deter the ambitious. No sooner had he left one young lady with her chaperon after a dance than he was besieged by prospective partners.

Lady Daphne stood up with him, and Maria Turner, the latter with the advantage of being both his hostess's daughter and his cousin's friend's sister. He waltzed with Mrs. Wilmington, the dashing, voluptuous widow he had snubbed in the Park—how had she coerced him into it? Thea wondered. She did not recognize two other damsels he led onto the floor.

Somehow he found Meg, surrounded by her own admirers, when the time came for the country dance she had promised him. He flashed Thea a smile as he neatly abstracted her sister from the group. She stopped worrying that he would forget her or search for her in vain, and started worrying that she would make a muddle of the newly learned waltz.

In the meantime, she danced a quadrille with Lord Stewart, grateful for his discreet reminders of the complicated figures. Will DeVine, resplendent in crimson velvet, requested a country dance. So did Sir Gideon Turner, who confided that he was desperately in love with Miss Megan.

"Ready to blow my brains out," he assured her solemnly.

"Don't do that!" she said in alarm, then recalled that his sister had told Meg he was given to impassioned attachments. "Meg may not favour you at present, but I doubt she will be ready to make up her mind before she has enjoyed the splendours of her Season in the spring. Though I am sure nothing could be finer than this ball," she added hastily.

"Promised Maria I'd do it up well. My only sister, you know, and she's not a bad chit. For a sister."

Thea was glad Meg did not favour him. He seemed a singularly brainless young man.

When Thea was not dancing, she stayed with Penny. Jason made a point of introducing his many friends and acquaintances to them. Thea was impressed by Penny's ability to converse with all and sundry despite never having met them before. She listened carefully, hoping to learn the knack, but decided the first requisite was a self-confidence she did not possess.

She did not understand how Penny could meet strangers with such tranquillity, yet be so unsure of herself when it came to her relationship with Jason. If love was to blame for so much unhappiness, Thea reflected, perhaps she was a widgeon to yearn for love.

"You are thoughtful, Miss Kilmore."

With a startled gasp she looked up at Roderick. He smiled at her and her heart quivered. Widgeon or no, she wanted more from the marquis than his friendship, precious as that was. Yet he must never guess, for if he came to consider her just another of the females who pursued him, her misery would equal Penny's.

He held out his hand to her. "It is time for our waltz, ma'am." As she rose and went with him to take their places, he said softly, "You are a trifle down pin, I think. Is this evening a great trial to you, Thea?"

"I find large numbers of people bewildering," she admitted.

"Nothing could be more natural after the solitude of the moors."

But how could she remain down pin or bewildered when his hand was at her waist, her hand in his firm clasp? She gave him a joyful smile as the music started and he guided her into the dance.

"Actually, so large a crowd is easier than a lesser company," she said to explain her sudden change of spirits, "since no one notices if I am tongue-tied."

"True. There is scarce space for the ladies to observe each other's gowns. The Turners' ball will certainly win the accolade of being described as a shocking squeeze."

"Accolade? How odd. The other advantage of a ball, I have discovered, is that during a country dance one spends little time with one's partner. It is only the waltz that is troublesome, for one is expected to do two difficult things at once—converse and mind one's steps."

"You seem to be managing remarkably well with both."

She realized that, swept along by his strong arm, she was indeed whirling about the floor without sparing a thought for her feet. He was a superb dancer, confident and graceful, as she had noticed when watching him earlier. However, his earlier partners had all been too short for him, forcing him to conform to their shorter steps, to bow his head to speak to them. For the first time in her life, Thea felt her height gave her a worthwhile advantage. If only they could waltz forever.

Roderick's blue eyes lit with rueful amusement. "I should not have spoken, since my words appear to have silenced you."

"Oh no, I was silently congratulating myself, since to do so aloud would be odiously conceited."

He laughed. "If there is one adjective I should never think to apply to you, it is *conceited*. Since you are in a mood to be pleased with yourself, let me say that yellow becomes you to admiration."

"You said that of my lavender dress."

"Are you accusing me of repeating myself? No punishment can be too dire for a gentleman so unoriginal as to offer the same compliment twice to a lady. The only possible explanation is that the admiration is owed to the wearer, who would grace any colour she chose."

Pink-cheeked, she retorted, "I see you are determined to *make* me conceited, sir. Pray let us talk of something sensible."

"By all means. What do you reckon are my chances of winning a wager that Princess Charlotte will be brought to bed of a girl?"

"Precisely one in two. But I said sensible! Have you really made so idiotic a wager?"

"No, but I wager half the gentlemen in this room have. At the clubs, it is quite the thing to bet on flies crawling on the wall, or raindrops running down the window-pane, or whether the next member to enter will wear a blue coat or a brown."

"And gentlemen are supposed to be the more-intelligent sex! Even Meg is wiser. At the Duchess of Trent's card party, she refused to play for more than penny points, though Penny was staking her. She said she kept thinking of all the ribbons and romantic novels she might buy with those shillings."

"Penny points at the Trents'?" The marquis grinned. "I wish I had seen it. And what did you do?"

"I sat and watched the whist players, pretending I wished to learn. Jason warned us that there is often deep play at the Trents'."

"Your brother was never a gamester, for all his other misdemeanours. Oh Lord, I beg your pardon—I ought not to have said that."

"I'm glad you did. I had not considered the possibility, but how shocking if he were to gamble away Penny's fortune."

"If he had been frequenting the gambling tables, I should have heard of it, no doubt. There is one less thing for you to tease yourself about."

Thea looked at him uncertainly. He had sounded almost irritated. "You must think me a peagoose to worry so much about my family."

"Not at all. I only wish..."

But what Lord Hazlewood wished was never voiced, as the music ended and they found themselves beside his cousin and Meg.

"Shall we go in to supper together, coz?" Mr. De-Vine suggested. "If you have no objection, Miss Kilmore. I can count on Rod to keep the hordes at bay, you see. I cannot think what possessed me to present my friends to Miss Megan."

Meg giggled.

"Is it time for supper?" Thea asked. "I should like to go with you, but perhaps Lord Hazlewood has arranged to take someone else in."

"That waltz was the supper dance, Thea," said her knowledgeable sister. "You go with your partner to supper."

So, as usual, Roderick had arranged matters for her comfort. She had felt the tiniest bit hurt that he had not danced with her earlier, but it was so that she would not have to sit through supper with an uncongenial partner, or none. Though she had to be grateful for his chivalrous forethought, she wished wistfully that he did not regard her merely as an object for his compassion.

She took his arm and all four proceeded to the supper-room.

The Turners' drawing-room and dining-room had been thrown into one for supper. Will had bribed a footman to reserve one of the tables set up in the drawing-room, a tiny table in a corner, barely large enough for four. He ushered Meg to the chair in the corner, telling her laughingly, "So that none of my rivals can approach you."

Before sitting down, Thea scanned the room. "I want to be sure that Penny has found a place," she explained to the marquis. "I cannot see her. Can you, sir?"

He turned from holding her chair and glanced around. "No. Would you like me to... Ah, there she is. With Kilmore and the Montmorencys."

"Thank you." She smiled at him as she took her seat. She could not regret his compassionate chivalry since it embraced Penny, too, who had real need of it.

There was no room for a buffet, so footmen with trays darted between the tables. Meg exclaimed in delight over lobster patties, truffled chicken *timbales,* chocolate wafers and raspberry ices. Her small appetite was soon satisfied, though, despite her exertions on the dance floor. While the others ate, she studied their fellow guests with a lively interest, commenting on a charming head-dress here, an intricately tied cravat there.

"And that gentleman's waistcoat far outshines yours, Mr. DeVine," she teased. "Peacock blue, with spangles and... Thea, I believe it is that man who was so rude to us at The Haycock. Do you remember? Ilminster, his name was. He took us for... for women of easy virtue."

"Ilminster insulted you?" Will half rose, his face matching his crimson coat, his knife clenched in his fist. "I'll horsewhip him!"

"You can't do that." Roderick laid a restraining hand on his cousin's arm.

"Then I shall call him out!"

"Pray do not," Thea begged.

"You might be hurt," said Meg, round-eyed.

"Sit down," the marquis commanded, and his cousin subsided. "You will draw everyone's attention, which is precisely why you will not challenge the earl. Do you want the entire beau monde whispering that Miss Kilmore and Miss Megan were mistaken for...er...ladies of easy virtue? You know such things cannot be kept quiet."

"Of course not, but how can you be so deucedly calm and collected about it? Forcing his attentions on innocent females!"

"Believe me, if it were not for the certainty of gossip, I should call out the scoundrel myself." The iron in his quiet, controlled voice and the fire in his eyes confirmed his words.

Thea blenched. Suppose he changed his mind, decided scandal could somehow be avoided? "Lord Ilminster was in his cups at the time," she said, attempting to excuse his behaviour. "I doubt he was able to... to force his attentions on anyone. Meg told him, 'Unhand me, sirrah,' and we left without harm."

Will gave a shout of laughter. Roderick grinned. "Did you really say that, Miss Megan?" he asked. "I once heard the line in a melodrama at The Haymarket, though I never supposed it might be pronounced anywhere but on the stage."

Meg twinkled at him. "Heroines in novels say it all the time. The villain generally leaves, uttering dire threats."

"I trust you will not rely on its efficacy, however. Real villains are rarely foiled by words not backed by the certainty of punishment."

"But you mean to let the infamous earl escape without punishment," Will complained.

"I shall give him the cut direct," said the marquis dispassionately, "and you will drop a quiet word in your friend Sir Gideon's ear to the effect that I do not care to frequent a house where Ilminster may be encountered. He will tell his mother, and if I am not mistaken, the earl will soon find himself *persona non grata* in respectable Society."

Will shook his head admiringly. "Since Lady Turner—along with half of Society's hostesses—harbours hopes that you will cast the handkerchief in her daughter's direction, I have no doubt but you are right.

Ilminster ran through his fortune years ago and cannot compare as a possible match.''

"As though Maria would marry Lord Hazlewood for his fortune," said Meg, filled with indignation. "Even if Lord Ilminster were twice as rich, she'd refuse him, because he is odious, and ugly, and wears dirty linen.''

"And a flashy waistcoat," pointed out the marquis, his gaze on Will's pale pink-and-white stripes.

"Oh, go to the...ahem...deuce, coz. Ah, people are returning to the ballroom. I'll go and have a word with Giddy. You know what he will say? 'The Divine Will has spoken.' And I'll tell him I'm backed by the Divine Rod....''

"Blasphemy," said his cousin severely, then he smiled at Thea. "With luck, after tonight you will no longer run the risk of coming face to face with the infamous earl. I hope you are satisfied with my solution?''

"Most certainly, sir. How dreadful it would be if he recognized us." Yet Thea wondered whether Lord Ilminster might not have preferred pistols at dawn to banishment from Polite Society. Will DeVine's wrath was violent, but Lord Hazlewood's was more to be feared, though he never allowed anger to ruffle his outward calm.

CHAPTER FOURTEEN

WEARING BLACK CRAPE in mourning for Princess Charlotte, Meg looked tinier than ever as she stood at the drawing-room window. She held aside one sage-green curtain with its border of bright autumn leaves and peered out into the dark. For once, no one chided her. "What shall we do?" she demanded yet again.

"I don't know," Penny wailed. "Tonight of all nights! I don't know if it will be worse to go without Jason or not to go at all."

"If I stay at home," the dowager volunteered, "the balance of ladies and gentlemen will not be upset. Mrs. Trevelyan will just have to remove two covers."

"If it were anyone but the Trevelyans, Mama," Thea reiterated patiently. Though her mother had not been told the full story, she knew enough to be aware that Alison Trevelyan had been singularly gracious to invite the Kilmores. How could Jason do this to his wife? "We shall be abominably late if we do not leave soon." She began to fasten the buttons of her slate-grey pelisse.

"I *cannot* face them without him." Penny paced, green eyes huge in her pale face, charcoal silk swishing about her ankles. Her hair flamed above the sombre colour. "Yet if neither of us goes—"

"Here he is!" Meg cried. She dashed for the hall door, Penny and Thea at her heels.

Dunmow, as anxious as his ladies, was loitering in the hall. He opened the front door and Jason came in, shaking raindrops from his beaver. Far from being apologetic, his expression was jubilant.

"Penny, it's all settled at last," he announced triumphantly. "Wait till I tell you—"

"Jason, we shall be late," Meg interrupted. "You are not even changed for dinner."

"Are we dining out?"

"Jason, the Trevelyans!" Penny moaned.

"To perdition with the Trevelyans! I cannot explain to you in company..." He realized his wife's lips were trembling, her eyes filling. "The Trevelyans? Yes, I suppose we must go. You take the carriage, my dear, and leave at once."

"I cannot go in without you."

"Of course not. Dunmow, have my horse brought round by a mounted groom. Five minutes! Penny, wait on the corner of Green Street until I come. I shall catch you up, I promise." He touched her cheek as he strode past to take the stairs two at a time.

He did not keep them waiting. Joining them in the carriage, he struggled out of his riding boots and put on evening pumps while Scargill drove the last few yards to the Trevelyans' house.

"I am not quite my usual immaculate self," he said, a laugh in his voice, "but I don't believe I smell of the stables after so short a ride. Come, Mama, let me help you down."

They were the last to arrive, but not so late as to cause comment. In fact, the only topic of conversation in the Trevelyans' drawing-room was the sad death of Princess Charlotte in the early hours of that morning, after bearing a stillborn boy.

The gentlemen spoke gravely of the political situation. The loss of the Prince Regent's only child left his brothers as his sole heirs. The youngest was in his forties, and not one of them had legitimate offspring. What was to become of the throne?

The ladies, all dressed in grey or black, talked in hushed voices of long and painful labour, of the Regent's disgraceful absence from his dying daughter's bedside. Many blamed her death on Dr. Croft's harsh regimen of bleeding and restricted diet. Penny looked more and more unhappy, and Thea began to wonder just how little her brother's wife had been eating of late.

She blamed herself for not observing Penny more closely. Occupied in chaperoning Meg, whose crowd of admirers constantly increased, and absorbed in her own emotions, she had neglected her sister-in-law. She moved towards her just as the butler announced dinner.

Since ladies and gentlemen had such different interests in Princess Charlotte, conversation at table of necessity turned to other subjects. Thea found herself flanked on one side by a Member of Parliament, who harangued her at length on the topic of Rotten Boroughs, and on the other by a young man more tongue-tied than herself. Neither required much of her attention. She watched Penny, some way down on the opposite side of the long table.

Mrs. Trevelyan had given Penny Lord Hazlewood for her dinner partner, but had seated her next to Jason. Looking worried, Jason abandoned his own partner to press titbits upon his wife. Penny made a valiant effort to eat, but she seemed to have completely lost her appetite.

The events of the evening had been more than enough to overset her, Thea thought. The prospect of visiting the Trevelyans, Jason's absence when she most needed his support, and then the talk of the princess's death in childbirth—no wonder Penny appeared far from well. If Jason did not have the sense to take her home immediately after dinner, Thea decided she would send a footman to drag him from his port.

Then she recalled that Jason had urgently wanted to talk to Penny. "It's all settled at last," he had said. What was settled? Was he going to explain what mysterious business had kept him from home all these long weeks? Curiosity gnawed at her.

At last Mrs. Trevelyan gave the ladies the signal to retire. Gentlemen stood as footmen moved to pull back chairs. With varying degrees of confusion as they gathered gloves and fans, the ladies rose. And then Penny dropped fan and gloves, raised her hand to her mouth, and swayed. Lord Hazlewood caught her as, eyes closed, she sank towards the floor.

Jason, who had at last politely turned to his partner, swung round. "Penny!" he cried and, fiercely possessive, seized her from the marquis's arms.

Alison Trevelyan was beside them in a flash, while Thea was still hurrying around the table. "Carry her to the library," she directed, and caught her butler's eye. "Lady Emma, if you would not mind . . ."

A smart woman of about thirty nodded. Jason, holding Penny close, followed the butler from the room. Mrs. Trevelyan swept Thea, Meg, and their mother along behind.

"I am so sorry, Mrs. Trevelyan," the dowager apologized in flustered distress. "Your dinner party . . ."

"Pray do not give it another thought, ma'am. Lady Emma will take the rest of the ladies to the drawing-room and I shall join them as soon as I know everything possible is being done to make Lady Kilmore comfortable. Oh dear, I hope nothing serious is the matter!"

"My sister-in-law is in the family way," Thea told her. "I suspect she was distressed by the talk of Princess Charlotte."

"No wonder! It was perfectly horrid."

They entered a room lined with bookshelves, where Jason was laying Penny on a sofa. Gently he raised her head to put a cushion under it and the dowager bustled forward.

"No, dear, keep her head down and raise her feet. Less elegant but far more efficacious." Taking charge, she lost her vagueness. From her reticule she produced a little bottle. "Thea, here is hartshorn. Mrs. Trevelyan, if I might trouble you for lavender water, and a little wine, and if possible a hot brick."

"Of course. I shall send for Mrs. Pugh, my housekeeper, and you shall have whatever you need." She gave orders to the butler. "And see that a chamber is prepared, with the bed warmed, lest Lady Kilmore needs to stay the night."

"No!" cried Jason. White with anguish, he was kneeling by the sofa, chafing Penny's hands. "Mama, she is not so ill as that, is she?"

"I hope not, dear. Thea, you can stop waving the vinaigrette. Her eyelids are fluttering. As long as she is not bleeding . . ." She cast an anxious glance at her silent younger daughter.

Mrs. Trevelyan promptly said to Meg, "Will you come with me to the drawing-room, Miss Megan? Between us we shall tell everyone in confidence that Lady Kilmore is *enceinte*, then no one will think anything of her faintness. Do you know, I once thought it would be prodigious romantic to swoon, but I see it is not at all as described in novels...." She and Meg went off arm in arm.

Thea silently blessed her. If Jason had once been in love with her, how could he ever have considered wedding Henrietta?

"Jason, go and stand by the door," his mother ordered. "Make sure no one enters for a moment."

"I don't want to leave her."

"Just for a moment, dear. You may be her husband, but this is women's business."

Unwillingly he obeyed. The dowager sighed with relief when she discovered no sign of blood on Penny's undergarments. Jason rushed back to her side just as she opened her eyes. She burst into tears and he took her in his arms.

Tears pricked Thea's own eyes. Blinking them away, she fetched the glass of wine the butler had poured from a decanter he'd placed on a small table. "Will she be all right, Mama?"

"I believe so, but rather than risk a miscarriage, she ought to spend the night here, since Mrs. Trevelyan has so kindly offered."

Penny overheard. "Jason, I want to go home," she wept.

"Then you shall, my darling. Mama, if I carry her, and she puts her feet up on the seat in the carriage...?"

The dowager acquiesced, took the wine from Thea, and urged Penny to drink. A little colour returned to her cheeks.

Thea went to answer a knock at the door and admitted the housekeeper, followed by a maid with a hot brick wrapped in a towel. Behind them stood Lord Hazlewood.

"How does Lady Kilmore go on?" he asked.

"Better, sir. Jason will take her home shortly. Have you seen my sister?"

"Miss Megan is conducting herself with admirable composure. She and Mrs. Trevelyan appear to be on the best of terms. Nonetheless, she looks a trifle woebegone."

Thea glanced over her shoulder at the group fussing about Penny. "I ought to go to Meg. Penny must keep her feet up in the carriage, so Jason will have to send it back for the two of us."

"I shall be happy to convey you both to Russell Square whenever you wish, but if I may make a suggestion, it will be best if you stay for a while."

"To keep people from talking? Yes, you are right. Just let me tell Mama, and I shall come to the drawing-room."

He waited for her, and she was glad to have him at her side when they entered, for most of the guests turned to stare.

Deserting two disconsolate young men, Meg sped to ask anxiously after Penny, and the Trevelyans came to join her enquiries. Mr. Trevelyan's genuine solicitude surprised Thea. Doubtless his wife had convinced him of the wisdom of putting aside his understandable animosity towards the Kilmores.

Reassured, Meg was recaptured by her new admirers. Lord Hazlewood and Mr. Trevelyan fell into a political discussion.

"It is an excessively political evening," Alison Trevelyan said apologetically to Thea. "Philip is a Member of Parliament, you see. I was sure everything would go wrong when I was entertaining so many important people, but he says I did just as I ought when your poor sister-in-law fainted. Will you come and meet Lady Lansdowne and the Cheverells? I believe you will like them."

Thea would have much preferred to find a quiet corner, but she agreed and was rewarded. The Marchioness of Lansdowne and Lord and Lady Cheverell, after expressing kindly concern about Penny, returned to talking about charities. They included Thea without pressing her to speak. She did like them, finding their conversation interesting, and when Lord Hazlewood joined them, she discovered they were friends of his.

She even ventured to ask some questions. Lord Hazlewood gave her an approving nod and no one sneered at her ignorance. A political evening, she decided, was a great improvement on a purely social occasion.

Taken by surprise when the tea tray was brought in, she exclaimed, "Is it so late? I did not mean to stay so long."

Lady Cheverell, an unpretentious woman of about Thea's age, smiled at her. "I am glad you did, Miss Kilmore. May I call tomorrow to ask after Lady Kilmore?"

Thea stammered out her direction, expecting the usual dismay, but the viscountess said, "Most convenient. Russell Square is on our way to the Foundling Hospital, is it not, Adam? Lord Cheverell and I are to visit there tomorrow, Miss Kilmore."

On the way home in Lord Hazlewood's carriage, Thea said with a sigh of satisfaction, "The evening did not turn out so badly in the end."

"How can you say so?" Meg demanded. "When Penny was taken ill like that!"

"She is not seriously ill." Thea kept to herself her near certainty that Jason loved Penny after all, since Meg had never been told that Penny doubted it. "And I met some most agreeable people, Lady Cheverell in particular. I never thought to feel so comfortable with strangers."

Lord Hazlewood said teasingly, "Perhaps because they 'have something to say,'" and Thea blushed as she recalled her earlier boast. He went on more seriously, "You have fallen into a nest of Whigs, Miss Kilmore, who are trying to better the lot of the poor, whether through Parliamentary action or private charity. Trevelyan was only recently converted to our way of thinking, by his wife, he claims."

"I like Mrs. Trevelyan immensely," said Meg. "She is only a year older than I am, and she has read all the same romantic novels."

The marquis laughed. "A firm foundation for friendship."

"Who were those two young gentlemen you were talking to, Meg?" Thea asked.

"Lord Frederick and Mr. Mills? Just two gentlemen," Meg said airily. "They asked permission to call."

"Have you met them before?"

"No, but they were properly introduced by Mrs. Trevelyan."

Thea sighed. Chaperoning Meg was no easy task when every young man she met proved susceptible to her charms. Thea had reached the conclusion that a proper introduction was unfortunately no guarantee of respectability. After all, Jason was received everywhere and had doubtless been properly introduced to Alison before he'd abducted her.

At least Meg's lack of fortune made that fate improbable, while also ensuring that few of her beaux were likely to become suitors.

As if he had read Thea's mind, Lord Hazlewood said, "I know no harm of Lord Frederick or Mr. Mills, unless political aspirations be considered a vice."

"They did not talk politics to *me*," said Meg.

"You surprise me," said the marquis drily as the carriage turned into Russell Square.

The dowager had already retired, the butler reported when the Misses Kilmore entered the house. His lordship was abovestairs, but had asked to be informed when his sisters reached home.

"Thank you, Dunmow, I shall tell him," Thea said. "How is Lady Kilmore?"

"Ever so happy, miss, if I may make so bold." The butler beamed. "You see, his lordship's found her old abigail, as was with her ladyship before and was her nurse before that. Mrs. Nancy arrived just this evening. Such a reunion, miss, it was a pleasure to see."

"How splendid of Jason!" Meg exclaimed. "To think he has been searching for Nancy all this time. Penny has often . . ." A huge yawn cut off her words.

"To bed!" said Thea. "Too many late nights and you will lose your sparkle."

They went upstairs together. Thea was delighted that Nancy had been found, but the search surely had not occupied all Jason's time. Nor did it explain his announcement that all was settled. She tapped on his dressing-room door as Meg retreated to her chamber, yawning again.

"Come in." Book in hand, a brown woollen dressing-gown over his shirt and pantaloons, he was sitting on a plain deal chair set close to the door to the bed-chamber. In one corner, the cot he had been sleeping on was turned down for the night, his nightshirt laid across it. A deal clothes-press and a cheap mirror completed the furnishings. Jason had given his wife a free hand, and he spent enough on his wardrobe to make a show in Society, but he had not spent a shilling of her money on his own comfort.

Thea had not been in his dressing-room before. She wondered whether Penny was aware of its Spartan simplicity.

He rose as Thea entered. "Ah, you are safely returned."

"How is Penny? Dunmow says you have found her Nancy."

"Yes, a month since. She had to work out her notice, and I didn't want to tell Penny in case something happened to prevent it. Penny is far happier to see her abigail than she was to see *me* when you came from Newkirk." He sounded tired and disheartened.

"Oh, Jason, she was ill and exhausted, and then to see the state of the house! But worst of all, you scarcely seemed overjoyed by her arrival. You told her she looked as if she had one foot in the grave, and you were not even pleased that she is pregnant."

"How can I care about an heir when she is ill?"

Buoyed by a successful evening, Thea took a deep breath and spoke her mind. "Apart from the morning sickness, which Mama says will pass, Penny is only ill because she is afraid you don't love her. She has been on a reducing diet to try to look more like Alison Trevelyan and Henrietta, since you admire them so much."

"*Once* admired them! They are pretty enough. Penny is beautiful."

"You have not told her she is beautiful, that you love her."

"I have," he said, indignant. "I told her both when I proposed to her."

Thea stared at him in shock. "That was months ago! You must tell her often, Jason. Particularly because of the...the unusual circumstances of your marriage, though I suspect all ladies need frequent reassurance. And instead, you have been absent from home most of the time since we came to Town."

"I have been working with her lawyers—our lawyers. I wanted to sort everything out quickly so that we can go back to Newkirk, since London does not agree with her."

"It is not London that disagrees with her, and I expect she would have liked to be consulted on the matter. Penny has a mind of her own."

He smiled wryly. "That I know. I did not wish to trouble her with business in her condition. I can see I was wrong. In any case, she has to approve all I have settled with the lawyers. Thea, they have agreed to almost everything I proposed, even—"

"I'm glad, but you can tell us all in the morning." She gave him a quick hug, then turned away and moved towards the door, feeling her face grow warm. "Now, forget your horrid cot and go and hold her in your arms."

His voice thick with longing, he said, "I must not disturb her rest when she is unwell."

"Jason, dear, that is the only way to make her well."

Thea escaped to her chamber. She couldn't wait to tell Roderick all about it, except—she put her hands to her hot cheeks—except for her final words of advice.

CHAPTER FIFTEEN

WHEN THE CHEVERELLS arrived, neither Penny nor Jason had come down yet, though the green-and-russet drawing-room was already well filled. Most of the callers were unattached gentlemen, from callow youths to the mature, if hardly venerable, figure of Mr. Glubb-ffoulkes.

"The Prince is sadly cast down," he said, a sigh making his corset creak, his hopeful gaze fixed on the box of bon-bons he had brought for Meg. "Rushed back from Suffolk as soon as he heard Her Highness was in labour, but he was too late to say goodbye to his daughter. Now he won't stir from his room, won't even dress, won't talk of anything but the late sad event."

Meg at once comforted and silenced him by opening his gift and setting it at his elbow. Maria Turner and Jane Lewin had come to visit her, escorted by Sir Gideon. Thea suspected that, while they liked her sister, they also hoped to profit from the overflow of beaux attending her.

Several ladies, unable to bring themselves to brave the wilds of Bloomsbury, had sent footmen to enquire after Penny's health. The house in Russell Square, though admittedly a disadvantage, was proving less than a disaster.

The Cheverells did not stay long, but Lady Cheverell invited Thea to call the next day. "Not just for a formal quarter of an hour," she said with a smile. "Come to tea and we shall have a comfortable cose."

Thea dared to hope that she had found a new friend, a rare and precious thing. She must tell Roderick. Where was he? Surely he would call today after last night's upset.

She looked up hopefully as Dunmow ushered in another gentleman. Lord Stewart entered and crossed the room to her side, his tread slightly ponderous though he was by no means a bulky man. The lines of grief on his face were less marked than when she had first met him, she thought. He was cheerful with her, and she had seen him laughing gaily while dancing with Mrs. Wilmington. The other day he had asked whether she had procured a riding habit yet—and that was another thing she wanted to talk to Roderick about.

In *his* presence, she would not mind making a cake of herself on horseback. She hoped he might go with her to one of the quieter parks to practise.

Lord Stewart proposed a drive in Hyde Park. Thea refused, luckily being provided with the excuse that she must stay with Meg. Their mother had gone to consult Lady Anne about Penny's health, physician-*accoucheurs* being in bad odour after Princess Charlotte's death.

The widowed viscount was still with her when Dunmow announced Lady Emma Osborne and Mrs. Trevelyan. Though pleased to see Alison Trevelyan, Thea was surprised that she had brought her older friend. Lady Emma seemed very proper and a trifle stiff.

"Miss Kilmore, is your sister-in-law recovered?" Mrs. Trevelyan asked anxiously.

"She is much better. In fact *everything* is much better," Thea said, trying to infuse her voice with meaning. "She is resting in her chamber today and my brother is sitting with her. I shall send to tell him you are come, for he would wish to thank you for your kindness last night."

The young Mrs. Trevelyan was no slowtop. "No, no, do not disturb them. He never loved me, you know," she said in a low voice, throwing a glance of sparkling mischief at Lady Emma. "We were friends, and one does not cast off a friend because of one mistake. He did not harm me in any way. I wish him well and I am very glad he has found happiness. Now I must go and have a word with Miss Megan."

Left with Lady Emma, Thea was once more at a loss. Lord Stewart conversed with her ladyship for a few moments, but he had stayed twenty minutes, so, always correct, he took his leave.

"It is obliging of you to call here, Lady Emma," Thea said shyly.

"I hope to call again, Miss Kilmore, when Lady Kilmore is receiving. You see, I eloped with an India nabob, so I have a certain fellow-feeling for your brother and his wife."

Astonished, Thea stammered, "Penny will be happy to receive you."

Lady Emma, her cheeks tinged with pink, made a complimentary comment on the drawing-room's colour scheme. Thea managed a stilted reply and Lady Emma's *savoir faire* carried them through the next few minutes. Then, at last, Dunmow announced Lord Hazlewood and Mr. DeVine.

They came straight to her and Mr. DeVine, after politely greeting Lady Emma, said with a smile, "Miss Kilmore, your mama tells us that Lady Kilmore is much more the thing this morning. I understand Rod had the honour of catching her when she swooned. To think that I have always avoided such political affairs, supposing them dull!''

"Dull? On the contrary. Though that bit was horrid, I found the rest of the evening interesting. Is Mama come home, then?"

"She left Arlington Street when we did, but she had to stop at an apothecary's, I collect, to purchase some nostrum Aunt Anne recommended. Tell me, is Miss Megan also newly enamoured of politics?"

"Hardly," said the marquis. "She informed us with considerable complacency that Lord Frederick and Mr. Mills did not talk politics to her. I see they are both here this morning."

His cousin glanced across at Meg and groaned. "So is Giddy, and Uncle Reggie appears to be making himself quite at home. Pray excuse me, ladies."

While the rest of Meg's admirers had been arriving and departing at the proper intervals, Sir Gideon, as his sister's escort, had stayed. Mr. Glubb-ffoulkes, with no acceptable excuse for his continued presence, had emptied the box of bon-bons and looked incapable of movement. He wheezed a cheery greeting to his nephew.

Lady Emma and the marquis chatted for a few minutes with the ease of old acquaintances, while Thea burned with impatience. At last Lady Emma caught Mrs. Trevelyan's eye and they left.

"Roderick, I have so much to tell you," Thea burst out, "but there are too many people here. Did you by any chance come in your curricle?"

"Are you inviting yourself for a drive?"

"Yes, if you have time? Only I cannot go unless Mama comes to chaperon Meg." She rang the bell for Dunmow, who reported that the dowager had returned and was abovestairs. Thea sent him to ask her mother to come down.

"There is one little problem I ought to mention," Roderick said gravely, but with a twinkle in his eye. "Will came with me, so he must walk home or outstay his welcome."

"Mr. DeVine is so agreeable a gentleman, neither Meg nor Mama will withdraw his welcome after a quarter of an hour. Indeed, I think it a very silly rule, for those who are determined to stay do so anyway." She cast a reproving glance at Mr. Glubb-ffoulkes, who winked at her.

"And the agreeable people, with whom one wishes to converse at length, politely take themselves off," the marquis added with a grin. "When you condemn men for foolish wagers, remember that morning calls are a female institution, with rules set by the ladies."

"At least morning calls do no harm," she retorted.

"I dispute that. Consider the rule that requires duty calls, on all sorts of petty occasions. When I think of the hours I have wasted in excruciating boredom . . ."

Laughing, she conceded the point and enquired, "I trust this is not a duty call?"

"Fishing for compliments? How could I possibly be bored when I never know what you will say next!"

Her mother's entrance saved her from having to respond. Reluctantly, the dowager agreed to take her daughter's place in the drawing-room. Roderick beckoned Will over and explained that he was to be stranded in Russell Square for an hour or so.

Brightening, Will looked back at Meg, but he obligingly set himself to entertain the dowager. Thea dashed off to fetch her bonnet and pelisse.

Peter, the new tiger, was proudly walking Lord Hazlewood's greys around the square. When he saw Thea, he delved into the pocket of his livery coat and thrust a smudged scrap of paper into her hands.

"Look, miss, look. Rosie writ me a letter. You 'member my Rosie, miss? You c'n read it if you want."

In crooked capital letters, Thea read, "DEAR PETER, YOUR AFFECT. SISTER ROSE."

A sudden memory brought tears to her eyes. She had been about Rosie's age when Jason went away to school. She had missed her big brother, had written to him, then gradually had adjusted to his absence.

"That is splendid, Peter," she said, returning the precious letter to the boy. She turned to Rod and said accusingly, "My lord, you have not been to Hazlemere recently!"

"True." He handed her into the curricle, took the reins from Peter, and joined her as his tiger jumped up behind. The temptation to tease was irresistible. "I fear I have been gadding about in Town, taking young ladies for drives in the Park, paying morning calls, dining out, and even dancing on occasion. A shocking waste of time."

"Oh dear, and I was going to ask you to waste some more time on me." Her guilty expression delighted him.

"You were?"

"To practise riding. It is so long since I was on horseback, I dare not ride in public lest I make a fool of myself. But I should not mind you seeing me."

He wasn't sure whether to be pleased or regretful that she was willing to look foolish to him. All too clearly, she did not regard him as a suitor—but then, he was not ready to regard himself as such.

Just because he was haunted by the memory of holding her trembling body in his arms, of a leaf in her hair and her soft lips so close; just because his heart lightened with joy at the sight of her, at the very prospect of seeing her—those were no reasons to kick over the traces and tie himself down for life. No good reason to mix his metaphors, either, he thought wryly.

"Why the sudden desire to ride again?" he asked with casual curiosity, turning into Great Russell Street.

"Lord Stewart keeps inviting me to ride with him."

A flash of furious jealousy startled him. *Was* he ready to regard himself as a suitor? He'd be damned before he gave his assistance for a rival's benefit. He summoned calm. "Surely your brother would be the best person to help you relearn the skills."

"Jason? Yes, I suppose so. Only I hate to tear him away from Penny now that all is going so well." She turned a joyful face to him, then blushed adorably and said with sudden shyness, "You recall what I told you? About Penny and Jason?"

"How could I forget?" He glanced warningly at Peter, perched just behind them and undoubtedly all ears.

She nodded. "Jason's absences were not what she feared. He told us all this morning. He has been working to persuade Penny's lawyers to let him spend some of her capital on improvements to Newkirk. They insisted on detailed figures of the prospective income, so he had to track down a number of landowners with similar properties and talk them into providing the information. That is why he was out at all hours."

"He has succeeded?" Only Thea's enthusiasm leavened Rod's utter boredom with the subject of Kilmore's finances.

"They will even sell out Consols enough to buy back two of the farms Papa sold." Her forehead wrinkled. "I am not perfectly sure what Consols are."

"Consolidated Funds, which are government bonds. A safe investment, much to a lawyer's taste."

"Oh." She sounded not much the wiser. "Anyway, the lawyers have also agreed to set aside two thousand pounds' worth of five-per cent Consols each for Meg and me. I know it is not a great sum, but do you not think that Meg will have more choice of suitors with a small dowry than with none?"

"It is too little to make any difference to a wealthy man, or to tempt fortune-hunters, happily. If she wished to marry a gentleman of small means—a vicar, say, or an aspiring politician—a hundred a year might turn the scales."

"Someone like Mr. Mills or Lord Frederick, you mean? I wonder whether I ought to try to discourage them. Meg has been used to making do with very little, but I should like to see her marry someone who can provide the comforts of life."

"My dear girl," he said, exasperated, "that is surely a matter for your mother and your brother to concern themselves with."

The hurt in her voice reproached him. "I do not mean to interfere, only Mama would not know how to go about rejecting a suitor, and Jason has other matters on his mind. Every moment he can spare from Penny, he vows to devote to perusing *Practical Observations on the Improvement and Management of Mountain Sheep.*"

Rod was going to explain that his annoyance was directed at Kilmore and the dowager, but they reached Oxford Street and a tangle of traffic absorbed his attention. As he steered the high-bred greys between hackneys, drays, elegant carriages and pedestrians apparently attempting suicide, he was very much aware of Thea sitting silently beside him. Why the devil had he chosen to drive down one of the busiest shopping streets in the world? By the time they reached Hyde Park, it would be time to turn around and go back.

The Tyburn Turnpike came into view. Traffic thinned and he turned into the Park. Few people were about. Perhaps the ton felt qualms about enjoying the fashionable promenade with Princess Charlotte not yet in her grave. Or perhaps it was simply the threatening clouds overhead that kept them away. Whatever the reason, Rod was glad that interruptions were unlikely.

"I'm sorry," he said. "What your mother and brother do is none of my business, and believe me, I do not think you interfering."

Her unhappy face cleared. "Then may I ask you something? Do you know whether Mr. DeVine has serious intentions towards Meg?"

"No, I have no idea." Once again she had taken him by surprise. "I doubt if he knows himself. He made your sister's acquaintance only a month ago, after all. Serious intentions take time to ripen."

"Do they? Yes, I daresay love at first sight is a myth propagated by those novels Meg reads. In that case, no doubt you cannot tell me whether Mr. Glubb-ffoulkes has serious intentions."

Noting the hint of mischief in her dark eyes, Rod laughed. "The only thing that could astonish me more than Uncle Reggie proposing would be Miss Megan accepting him." He decided he ought to put in a good word for his cousin. "She could do worse than Will, however. Not only is he well to pass, but equally important, his estate, Goff's Acre, is in Hertfordshire, less than twenty miles from London. She would never have to endure a long journey.''

She smiled. ''A point worth considering if your cousin should decide to press his suit.''

She consulted him seriously about the eligibility of several young men, and he did his best to answer. After a quick circuit of the Park, they started back towards Bloomsbury.

''Was that why you inveigled me into deserting Will?'' he asked when she ran out of Meg's suitors.

''That, and the news of Penny and Jason, and the riding practice, and there was something else. What was it? Oh, Lady Cheverell. She has invited me to tea tomorrow, for the kind of conversation one cannot have during a morning call. I like her so much.''

''Yes, she is an amiable lady, and charitable. Her father was a country vicar, I believe, and her brother also.''

''Really? How odd that Society considers itself so exclusive, yet I keep meeting people with quite commonplace connections. How can anyone look askance at Penny? Why, Lady Emma Osborne herself just told me she eloped with an India nabob.''

''An aspiring politician of far from meagre means.'' Rod did not comment—lest it should make her self-conscious—that Thea was beginning to have a most satisfactory acquaintance among the ton. In time, he thought, she might even overcome her bashfulness with strangers. ''As for the riding,'' he went on, ''I can take you out once or twice, but I find business calls me to Hazlemere next week.''

''Cor, d'you mean it, guv?'' Peter burst forth. He had held his tongue admirably until now.

Thea turned her head to smile at the boy. "I'm so glad," she said, then turned back to Roderick. "Will you . . . will you be gone long?" she added wistfully.

"A few days." Was she going to miss him? Or was she only afraid that during his absence some problem would arise for which she needed his help?

CHAPTER SIXTEEN

CHOCOLATE BROWN, with apricot braiding, the severely cut habit was as becoming to Thea as Penny had envisaged it. Lord Stewart actually exclaimed in admiration as Thea descended the stairs. He seemed unable to drag his gaze from the spot where the apricot ostrich plume, curling around the small, neat hat, kissed her cheek.

It tickled, but she managed to restrain herself from twitching. "One must suffer in the cause of beauty," Meg had told her sternly.

To spare her riding horseback through the busy streets, Lord Stewart had brought his phaeton to drive to Hyde Park. They met his groom there. Thea was charmed by the pretty strawberry roan mare he had provided for her. Confident after her practice sessions with Roderick, she accepted with aplomb the viscount's help in mounting.

Though the day was fine for mid-November, the Park was far from crowded. At ease on the well-behaved mare, Thea reminisced about long-ago pony rides across the moors, where one had always to be wary of bogs and rabbit holes and sudden mists rolling in from the west. She amused Lord Stewart with vivid descriptions of the agony of taking a toss into a furze bush, and the relief of landing in springy heather.

"Miss Kilmore, how well you understand the pleasures and pains of childhood," he said fervently when they were once more seated in the phaeton. "I respect you for considering your empathy with youthful sensibilities more important than preserving your dignity as a lady of fashion."

Thea opened her mouth, then closed it again, unable to think of any suitable response. She ought to have known that talking freely to anyone but Roderick was a mistake. Nothing could be more undignified than falling off a horse into a gorse bush, even if it had happened a dozen years ago. In future, Lord Stewart would always picture her as a sad romp rather than an elegant, decorous lady.

What a shocking waste of her beautiful new habit!

On the other hand, he had indubitably expressed approval, of a sort. The possibility dawned on her that he was seeking not just a sympathetic ear, but a new mother for his children. He was actually considering her, Thea Kilmore, as a bride.

She hardly knew him! She hadn't yet even sorted out how many children he had. In a quiet panic, she tried to concentrate on what he was saying now, something about the busy streets that required no answer, thank heaven. He was an undemanding, solicitous companion, but...

A street urchin ran up to the phaeton, threw something into her lap, and dashed away, disappearing into an alley. Thea caught the twist of paper as it slid down her skirts.

Lord Stewart frowned. "What is that? The lower classes become more impudent every day."

Puzzled, Thea smoothed it. There was no superscription. She unfolded the sheet and silently read the impatient scrawl: "Tell my niece I need five thousand guineas and she will be sorry if I dont get it."

No names, nothing to incriminate the sender, but she knew at once that Mr. Vaughn had penned the demand, and the threat. She shivered.

"Miss Kilmore, what is it?"

"Nothing. A...a childish prank, I daresay." Wadding the paper into a ball, she unconsciously began to tear it into little pieces with nervous fingers. To tell Lord Stewart would solve nothing. She refused to upset Penny. Jason could do nothing if he knew, since Mr. Vaughn had given no direction, no instructions for paying the money.

All she wanted to do was run to Roderick, but he was at Hazlemere. The burden was hers alone.

THAT NIGHT the image of Mr. Vaughn's hulking menace, fist raised, kept her awake for hours. When at last drowsiness overcame fear, memory conjured up Roderick's arms about her. His gentle strength enfolded her as he held her close with murmured words of comfort. As she drifted into fantasy, his words grew tender and passionate, his blue eyes glowed as they had that windy day in St. James's Park, when she thought he was going to kiss her...

But in the morning she was alone again, with Mr. Vaughn's note an ominous weight on her mind.

As days passed and no more was heard of him, she began to hope the threat was an empty gesture. She decided not to mention it to Roderick when he returned from Buckinghamshire. To trouble him with her vague fears could only confirm his view of her as a weak, dependent creature thrown into high fidgets by the least little problem. In view of the strange method of delivery, perhaps the paper had not been meant for Penny after all, and its appropriate message was a coincidence.

Penny and Jason's renewed happiness filled the house. Meg revelled in the ever-increasing invitations, the assemblies, balls, and routs where she was always surrounded by admirers. The dowager smiled gently and went her own way, correcting her daughters when she felt they needed it, but spending more and more time with Lady Anne, helping her to index her work.

"A MORE UNLIKELY PAIR I never saw," Will observed to his cousin one night as they lingered over a glass of brandy in the library after an evening at the theatre. "Aunt Anne says the Dowager Lady Kilmore writes a neat hand and can spell obscure medical terms, but why she should choose to act as amanuensis, I cannot imagine."

"Miss Kilmore told me her mother is used to a busy life, yet she dislikes the usual occupations of a fashionable matron in Town." Rod grimaced. "Unfortunately, those occupations she avoids include chaperoning her daughters."

"Unfortunately Meg . . . Miss Megan is deuced well chaperoned, by her sister and swarms of beaux. I never have her to myself."

"You've swallowed the bait, have you? I wondered."

"She's hooked me," Will confessed, refilling his glass. "Perhaps because she casts out no lures, so one forgets to be wary."

"She appears to have no need to employ tricks."

"True, but it's more that she's enjoying herself too much to have any present interest in catching herself a husband. Somehow I must get her away from the crowds. You wouldn't mind if I married her?''

"My dear coz, why the devil should I?''

"After all, I am your heir, though I'm not likely to inherit, thank heaven, as you are only half a dozen years older than I.''

"Eight years. Thank heaven?''

"Damned if I know what I'd do with that great pile of yours. I much prefer Goff's Acre.'' Suddenly he sat bolt upright, spilling a few drops of brandy on his blue-and-gold-brocade waistcoat. "I have it! Christmas at Goff's Acre. I shall have a house party.''

Rod grinned. "A house party for two? Just you and Miss Megan?''

"I shall have to invite her family, alas. Lady Kilmore seems to be fit as a fiddle now. Rod, you will come, will you not? You can keep Miss Kilmore occupied for me. And Stewart is showing signs of interest there. I'll ask him, too. Between the two of you, she won't have time to watch Miss Meg too closely.''

Stewart! Could he nowhere escape the damnable fellow? Rod was jealous, he was forced to admit—to himself. Will seemed to have no notion of his cousin's warm feelings for Thea, but he might guess if Rod objected to inviting the viscount. Hoping that Lord Stewart would choose to spend Christmas with his children, he asked, "Who else?''

Will pondered. "Aunt Anne, as nominal hostess and to entertain the dowager. My aunt Hazlewood is going to one of your sisters as usual, I trust?''

"Amelia has that honour this year, I believe.''

"Thank heaven. In that case, I'll invite Uncle Reggie. Don't want to hurt the old boy's feelings, and he'll liven things up.''

"You don't regard him as a rival, I collect."

"For Meg's hand? *Uncle Reggie?* Besides being sixty and fat as a porpoise, he's even more expert at avoiding parson's mousetrap than you are. Let's see, that is almost all family, mine and hers. It will be dull as ditchwater for you. Shall I ask Lady Daphne, or Mrs. Wilmington, to amuse you?"

"Heaven forbid! How about the Cheverells?" Rod knew that Thea and Lady Cheverell were becoming fast friends.

"No, no, coz. I'm not turning my house party into one of your political gatherings! And I don't want Giddy around casting sheep's eyes at Meg, or I'd ask the Turners. She is thick as thieves with Giddy's sister."

"How about the Lewins, then? Miss Lewin is a friend of Miss Megan's, is she not?"

"Yes," said Will decisively, "and Pretty's *épris* in Jane Lewin's direction, if I'm not mistaken. How he can prefer her to Meg escapes me, but he'll make up the numbers nicely. I shall be betrothed by the New Year and wed before Easter."

"Don't count your Easter eggs before they hatch," Rod advised his exuberant cousin, but he was wondering if a week at Goff's Acre might not be just what he needed.

In such limited company, Thea could have no possible reason for calling on his help or advice. He knew now that he wanted her for his wife, but he didn't want her to marry him only to have someone to turn to in times of trouble.

At least, with Thea, he had no fear that all she cared for were his title and his money. Whether he was willing to settle for less than love, if necessary, he was far from certain.

THE NEXT MORNING he went to see his lawyer and his banker, and then, still in a mood of unwonted confusion, he rode out to Hampstead. Sue was surprised to see him on a dank, drizzling afternoon. Setting aside her sewing, she rang for tea, poked up the fire, then settled to give him her full attention.

Instead of taking his usual place in the chair opposite hers at the fireside, Rod leaned on the mantel and stared down into the flames flickering about the glowing coals. "I'm going away for Christmas," he said, "and I may not be back."

He heard her stifled gasp before she faltered, "*May* not?"

"I've found the woman I want to marry."

"Surely you cannot suppose she would be foolish enough to reject you," she said with tolerable composure. "Who is she?"

"Thea Kilmore."

"I thought it might be. You have spoken of her more than of anyone but your mother. I almost feel I know her." She hesitated. "As you have described her, I cannot quite picture her as a marchioness, running Hazlemere and the Town house, entertaining your political associates, and so on. Is that why you are uncertain?"

"No. I shouldn't expect her to become a *grande dame* overnight, if ever. Indeed, I sincerely hope she will not if it means taking a leaf from my mother's book." He turned from the fire and took his seat as Enid brought in the tea tray. Sue poured as he continued. "Many women leave the management of a large household entirely to servants while they occupy their lives with fashion and gossip. Let Thea cultivate her kitchen garden should she so choose!''

"And your friends?''

"She is already on good terms with several of their wives. If she finds it too difficult to act as hostess for large, formal gatherings, we shall have small, informal parties, which I prefer anyway.''

"Does not your position demand entertaining on a grand scale?''

"My position allows me to do as I wish—within reason—and my wife likewise. You know my mother's invitations are the more prized because they are rare. But in any case, Thea's confidence is growing as she comes to know people and feels more at home with the ways of Society. She is no coward, Sue. When I recall how she faced Lady Kilmore's uncle . . .''

"Yes, you told me. You said you came nearer to losing your temper with that man than you have since you were a child.''

Rod grinned. "I was seven. I lost my temper with one of my sisters when she said a hedge was too high to jump, so I set my pony at it, though I knew she was right. The pony made it, with a few scratches. I didn't. I broke my leg and couldn't ride at all for months. A painful and compelling way to learn that to lose control of one's emotions is to lose all discretion.''

"So with your usual calm you sent to the rightabout the villain who threatened Miss Kilmore, and you believe the courage she showed then will help her to take her place as your wife. Then what is the difficulty? Do you truly think she may refuse you?''

"If I say no, I shall appear a shocking coxcomb.''

"Oh, fustian, Roderick! Only a complete ninny-hammer would turn you down, and you would not have fallen in love with a complete ninnyhammer."

"No, but you will have gathered that since the moment I met her I have rescued her—or more often her family—from any number of predicaments." He set down his empty teacup and crossed to a sideboard where decanters stood ready. A glass of Madeira in hand, he returned to the fire and once again took up his pose, staring into the flames. "She runs to me for assistance and advice. Is it too much to hope that she might some day come to see me as more than a knight errant?"

Sue rose and moved to his side. Her arm about his waist, she leaned her head against his shoulder. "If she does not, she is indeed a fool," she said quietly, a note of pain in her voice. "In that case, you will not marry her?"

"I don't know." His doubts remained unresolved. "I want her love!"

"Give her time, Rod. You have known her only a few weeks."

"You are right, of course. That's more or less what I told her when she asked whether Will is seriously attempting to fix his interest with her sister. Although, as a matter of fact, he is. That is his purpose in holding a house party over Christmas."

"Which is where you are going?" She shivered, though they stood right before the fire.

He embraced her briefly, then let her go. She sat down, her hands tightly clasped in her lap.

"I'm sorry, my dear."

"It was bound to happen sooner or later," she said dully. "I always knew it, but as time passed I have allowed myself to forget."

"You shall never be forced to...to find someone else," Rod said, taking a packet of papers from his pocket and placing it on the tea tray. "After we have been faithful to each other for so many years, I would not betray the bonds of friendship, of affection between us, in that way. Here are the deed to the house and documents relating to an annuity that will keep you in comfort all your life."

Sue nodded, not touching the packet. Her gaze on his face seemed to burn through him. "You will be faithful to her," she whispered, "as you have been faithful to me. Now go. Don't come back, ever. I could not bear it."

He bent to kiss her forehead, then strode from the room, from the house. Until that moment, he had not guessed that she loved him. Could the ten good years possibly atone for the pain of parting? Turning north, into the country, he rode Achilles long and hard through the rain.

THAT NIGHT, at the Cheverells', he waltzed with Thea. Floating in his arms in a cloud of cerulean blue net, she sparkled in response to his forced cheerfulness. Yet at the end of the dance she said with sweet concern, "You are troubled, are you not, my lord?"

"I hoped I was hiding it!"

"I daresay no one else has noticed. If you prefer, I shall say no more. Only, you have often listened to my troubles, and I know sometimes a sympathetic ear helps to put things in perspective. So, if you wish to talk..."

Her solicitude warmed him. He yearned to unburden himself, but Sue might well be the only subject he could never, ever discuss with Thea—just as he ought not to have discussed his love for Thea with Sue. Nor would he have, had he realized the depth of her feelings and how his words must hurt her.

"But I do not mean to pry," Thea finished anxiously.

"Of course not. I am not unacquainted with your eagerness to soothe others' woes." He had to tell her something. "I have made someone unhappy, someone of whom I am fond."

"Oh dear, how very distressing. Is there nothing you can do to remedy matters?"

"Nothing."

"Can I help?"

"I fear not." Over her shoulder, he saw Lord Stewart approaching. He smiled at her. "You must not worry, Miss Kilmore. Servant, Stewart."

"The next dance is mine, I believe, Miss Kilmore," said the viscount with a hint of belligerence.

"Yes, it is, sir. Is it already time to form the sets? Have you by any chance seen Megan? I hope she has not been looking for me."

Lord Stewart peered round to no effect. Rod, with the advantage of his greater height, told her, "Miss Megan sat with your brother and Lady Kilmore during the waltz. She is about to stand up for the country dance with Sir Gideon Turner if my eyes do not mistake me."

Thea thanked him with a smile and Stewart cast him a glance of envious annoyance. She went off on the viscount's arm, but Rod was left with a feeling of satisfaction quite out of proportion to his petty victory over his rival.

For once she had tried to help him, instead of the other way about.

HE WAS DISAPPOINTED to learn from Will that Lord Stewart had accepted the Christmas invitation. At least, forewarned, he was first to offer to drive Thea to Goff's Acre.

Will had pointed out hopefully that Miss Megan might withstand the horrors of travel better in his curricle than in a closed carriage. For so short a journey, the dowager judged that unexceptionable. So, two days before Christmas, a cavalcade set out from Russell Square.

As host, Will left first, with Megan beside him bundled in a cocoon of rugs. Then the Kilmore carriage bore off Lord and Lady Kilmore, the dowager, and Lady Anne. At the last moment, Thea discovered she had left her muff abovestairs. She hurried to her chamber to fetch it, her abigail having left earlier with the other personal servants and the baggage.

Waiting in the hall, Rod recalled his first visit to the house, which he had made with the laudable aim of saving the Kilmore sisters from oblivion. He could hardly blame Thea for seeing him as a white knight when he had played the part to the hilt. Yet even then he had been attracted to her as much by her pluck as her vulnerability.

He looked up as she came down the stairs, pink-cheeked and laughing. Even the warm cloak could not disguise her graceful slenderness. Now he desired her as he had never desired a woman before, but he wanted love, not gratitude, to bring her to his arms.

"Pray do not tell Meg I kept you waiting," she begged gaily as they started down the front steps to the street. "How she would roast me!"

A ragamuffin darted up to them. His face was half hidden by an aged hat pulled down over his eyes, a tattered collar turned up about his chin. "You Lady Kilmore?" he demanded.

"No, she has gone into the country. I am Miss Kilmore." Thea's voice shook and she clung to Rod's arm.

"You'll 'ave ter do. 'Ere." The boy thrust a piece of paper at her and was off before Rod could react.

She dropped it. Bending to pick it up, he read the scrawl on the outside: PENELOPE. He frowned as he handed it to her.

"You know what this is, Thea?"

"Please, let us go." She scanned the square fearfully and hurried to the curricle. As Peter scrambled up behind and Rod set the horses in motion, she broke the seal and read the contents. "I shall *not* give it to Penny," she said, her face pale.

"Her uncle?"

"Another threatening demand for money, this time with instructions on where to deliver it." She tore it in half, and in half again.

"Another! Why have you told me nothing of this?"

"What could you have done? You were at Hazlemere when the first was thrown to me in Lord Stewart's carriage, in the street. It had no names, no direction. When nothing happened I hoped it was a mistake."

"Nonetheless, I wish you had told me." He was being unreasonable, he knew—dissatisfied when she came to him for help, affronted when she did not. "Never mind, Vaughn will hardly pursue his niece into Hertfordshire, so forget his bluster. I wager it is no more than that.''

He set himself to amuse her, and before long was rewarded with the return of colour to her cheeks and a smile to her sensitive mouth. The shadow in her eyes remained.

CHAPTER SEVENTEEN

"PRINNY HAS LEFT off his stays," announced Mr. Glubb-ffoulkes. His plate laden with a second helping of nearly everything from the luncheon buffet, he lowered himself creakily to his seat opposite Thea. "Says he don't have the heart to bother since Charlotte died. A frightful sight, he is, with his belly down to his knees."

Seated beside him, Meg giggled. Will, on her other side, groaned. "Uncle, not at table, if you please!"

"Not to worry, my boy, I've no intention of giving up my corsets. Daresay puss here wouldn't care for it." He beamed at Meg.

"Pray, sir, keep them on. I think the Cumberland corset a wonderful invention."

"You're a good girl. Tell you what, since you don't favour my suit, you ought to have a go at one of the royal dukes. They are all casting off their mistresses and running after German princesses, the jobbernowls, hoping to beget an heir. Don't know what they're missing at home."

"Uncle, if you dare bring Miss Megan to the attention of any of those reprobates . . ."

"Why, perhaps Miss Meg has a fancy to be Queen," protested the old court-card with a twinkling glance at Thea.

Will's reaction confirmed what Thea had already guessed. Only his serious interest in Meg explained the house party, with the guests all friends of the Kilmores. Nor had she missed the fact that he had omitted all his rivals from his list, save Mr. Glubb-ffoulkes, who scarcely counted. Meg had told her she favoured Will, though no one could have guessed from her demeanour that she liked him any better than the rest of her court.

Since Thea dared not hope for any closer connection with Roderick, she thought wistfully that marriage between her sister and his cousin would be some consolation.

As THE DAYS PASSED, the pleasures of Christmas chased Mr. Vaughn's threats from Thea's mind. She joined in gathering evergreens, holly and mistletoe to garland the house. She helped choose a yule-log and cheered on the gentlemen as they dragged it to the house. Carols in the little church in the village of Goff's Oak; roast goose, mince pies, and flaming plum pudding; servants, tenants, and tradesmen crowding in with cheerful faces for their Christmas boxes on Boxing Day; excursions to Hatfield House and Waltham Abbey: Will was determined to entertain his guests in fine style.

Between the various amusements, Thea enjoyed her return to the peace of the countryside. The company was small enough, and well enough known to her, to give her no cause for uneasiness. Lord Stewart and Roderick were flatteringly attentive, though Meg said something that suggested Will had asked the marquis to keep her chaperon-sister occupied.

Expecting no better, Thea settled for the joy of riding with him through snowy woods and fields, sitting beside him at the informal meals, playing backgammon with him in the evenings. Though Lord Stewart usually tagged along as an unwanted third, she was happy, so she treated him kindly.

Will had planned a ball on New Year's Eve, the day before the house party was to break up. Thea was looking forward to it until she realized he had invited dozens of friends and neighbours. Somehow the brief absence from the haunts of the ton had renewed her apprehension at the thought of meeting strangers, her fear of doing or saying something wrong. Even her new ball gown, a dark wine red with white lace trimmings and flounces, seemed far too dashing.

As guests began to arrive, she hid behind a bank of red-berried yew and sweet-smelling pine branches in the ball room. The musicians from the village were already tuning up when Rod, a glass in his hand, found her lurking there.

"I know I shall make a mull of it," she wailed in despair. "I shall ruin everything for Meg."

"Nonsense." He sat down beside her, his sheer size a protective bulwark. "Here, drink this champagne and you will feel much better."

"Do you think I ought? I am not much used to wine."

"I am certain you ought. You must have heard the terms Dutch courage and pot-valiant."

"Not spoken with approbation, however!"

He smiled. "One glass can do no harm. Why do you say you might ruin everything for Meg?"

"Because I suspect Mr. DeVine has gathered his friends and neighbours with the hope of announcing his betrothal. He has been acting in a positively proprietorial way towards Meg these past few days. Do you not think it possible?''

''In confidence, more than possible. Will told me he has received permission from your brother to pay his addresses.''

''That is splendid!'' Raising the glass in a silent toast, she sipped the champagne. Bubbles tickled her nose as the wine slid down her throat like silk. ''So you see, I do not want to spoil the evening for Meg by making a *faux pas*.''

''My dear girl, why the deuce should you make a *faux pas*? You have been consorting with the beau monde for weeks now without a slip of the tongue, let alone any unacceptable conduct.''

''But there are so many people here I do not know.''

''None are in the least likely to threaten you with bodily harm, as did Vaughn, and you managed to stand up to him most valiantly.''

The comparison struck her. ''And I was not even pot-valiant, since for breakfast I drank nothing stronger than tea.''

''I should hope not!''

''But I was terrified.''

''Whereas now you are merely bashful.'' He gently removed the empty glass from her fingers, stood up, and offered his arm. ''May I beg the honour and the pleasure of the first cotillion, ma'am? I have a wish to be seen standing up with the most elegant female in the room.''

She rose and laid her hand on his arm. ''Do you like my gown?'' she asked shyly.

''It is superb.''

''Penny chose the colour, and it is so unusual I was not sure. . . .''

"Lady Kilmore has an unerring eye, but even she could not create such a dazzling effect were beauty not there to be adorned."

The champagne bubbles sang in Thea's head. "That is the nicest compliment I have ever received," she said. She was sorely tempted to throw her arms about his neck and cry aloud, *"I love you,"* but that would cause just the sort of scene she dreaded. Already they were surrounded by couples taking their places in the sets for the cotillion.

The familiar steps of the dance further raised her confidence. Glancing about, she saw Meg and Will in a nearby set, laughing with each other. Meg's eyes sparkled as brightly as the silver stars embroidered on her white net overdress.

Penny and Jason stood under the archway to the supper-room. Penny's figure was visibly thickening now, but Jason's arm was about what was left of her waist and he had eyes for no one else. As Thea watched, he pointed at a bunch of mistletoe hanging from the arch above them, and when Penny looked up, he kissed her.

"A pleasing sight," said Roderick, following Thea's gaze. "I trust they are grateful for your part in their *rapprochement.*"

"Mine? All I did was explain their misunderstanding to Jason." She blushed as she recalled ordering her brother to his wife's bed.

Roderick regarded her quizzically, but to her relief the dance came to an end with a final flourish from flute and fiddle. Instead of asking the cause of her blush, which she knew him quite capable of doing, he requested the supper dance.

Lord Stewart was waiting for her as they strolled to the side of the room. "I had hoped to have the first dance with you, Miss Kilmore," he said, slightly disgruntled. "I looked for you but could not find you." He stared suspiciously at the marquis.

Thea hated to see him in the mopes. Gladly granting his request for the next country dance, she did her best to cheer him up while they waited for it to begin. He soon regained his spirits and partnered her with his usual agreeable manners.

Will DeVine, her next partner, congratulated her with a grin. "You charmed Stewart out of the sullens very neatly." Observing her surprise, he hastily retracted his comment. "Dash it, I beg your pardon. That sounds calculating, and I know you and your sister to be the least calculating of females. I've never met a girl as unaffected as Meg . . . Miss Megan," he confided, smiling fondly at his beloved, a few places down the set.

By the time the supper waltz came round, Thea had stood up with Jason, Mr. Pritchard, two local gentlemen who had begged Will for introductions, and a second time with Lord Stewart. She had not sat out a single dance, and enjoyed even those with the two strangers.

The only thing to mar her pleasure was that Roderick had also stood up for every set, with the prettiest ladies in the room, it seemed to Thea. Knowing he had been as polite, as amiable, as charming to each as he was to her, she thanked heaven that she had resisted the temptation to reveal her love.

Banishing her chagrin with an effort, she smiled up at him as he led her onto the floor. He was quite the handsomest man present, and no one else knew that he had only requested a second dance out of kindness.

They did not talk as they whirled about the room. Light as a bubble, she swayed and swirled to his lead, the floor intangible beneath her satin slippers. Aware only of his blue eyes, the strength of his arm at her waist, she was bewildered when the music stopped.

"Dizzy?" he asked with the sympathetic amusement that always heartened her. "Come and eat something, and you will soon feel more the thing."

Together they joined the crowd heading for the supper-room. Still in her bubble, Thea saw Meg and Will ahead of them, surrounded by gentlemen begging to share their table. As the pair reached the archway, Will stopped and tenderly kissed Meg's cheek.

The young fellows around them applauded. "Mistletoe!" "A kiss!" "Give us a kiss, Miss Megan," they cried. And Meg, laughing, offered her cheek to one and then another, while Will stood by, his face like a thundercloud.

"I WAS ONLY HAVING FUN," Meg wept, still trying the next morning to explain how she had come to deeply offend her suitor. "I did not mean anything by it. I love him! How was I to guess he would be so dreadfully angry?"

Her mother rocked her. "You hurt him, dearest. Not that he did not have a right to be angry, for your behaviour was shocking."

"I know. I'm sorry, Mama. What shall I do? I don't want to marry anyone but Will."

"Don't despair, Meg," Thea advised. Perched on the end of the bed, she regarded her sister's tear-blotched face with deep sympathy. She perfectly understood how a moment's lack of forethought could lead to disgrace. "Mr. DeVine is—"

A tap on the door interrupted her. Meg's abigail came in, bearing a tray with a pot of tea and three cups. "There you are, my lady. There's nothing like a cup of tea. Oh, my poor Miss Megan!" She seemed about to burst into tears in turn, but pulled herself together. "Miss Thea, Lord Stewart's asking after you. He's in the library if you can spare him a minute."

Thea had a sinking feeling she knew what the viscount wanted.

"Go along, dear," said her mother. "I daresay Meg will sleep for a while when she has drunk her tea. She had little enough rest last night and she has the journey home to face this afternoon."

Reluctantly Thea left her sister's chamber and started down the stairs. Before she was halfway down, Will DeVine appeared in the hall below her. He was almost as wan as Meg, but he summoned up a smile that was a shadow of his usual jaunty grin.

"Miss Kilmore, may I have the pleasure of driving you back to Town this afternoon?"

Thea hesitated. He was asking her so that Meg could not possibly expect him to take her up in his curricle. On the other hand, he was willing to drive one of her family, which was surely a hopeful sign. He could have offered the place to Jane Lewin, or even his Aunt Anne or Uncle Reggie, if he wished to cut his connection with the Kilmores. Perhaps she might venture to speak on Meg's behalf.

"Thank you, sir, I shall look forward to it."

He bowed and moved aside, and she continued on to the library.

Lord Stewart stood at a window, gazing out at the melting snow in the garden. He jumped visibly when Thea spoke his name.

"My dear Miss Kilmore." Turning, he hurried towards her. "How good of you to grant me a few minutes when I know you wish to be soothing your sister's sorrows. I would not have requested a meeting but that I am going home for a few weeks, not back to London. It is my dearest wish that you—and your family, of course—will soon join me there to meet my children."

"To meet your children?" Thea repeated stupidly.

"I am saying this very badly. Believe me, it is no easier to propose a second time than it was the first! Miss Kilmore, your gentleness, your modesty, and especially the kind way you look after your young sister's welfare have convinced me that I cannot hope to find a better mother for my poor orphans. Nor am I insensible of your charm and beauty. I most sincerely offer you my hand and my heart."

Though Thea had been half expecting an offer of marriage, her knees felt weak. She sank onto a chair and endeavoured to collect her thoughts. The viscount was a pleasant, personable man. His devotion to his children—she still was not sure how many he had—bore out her impression of his kindly nature. However, if she wed him, she might well find herself playing second fiddle. Was it worth it, to have a home and family of her own?

Jason and Penny would welcome her to live with them, and she loved them dearly. Yet she would always be a poor relation, playing second fiddle there, too. A spinster of five and twenty, with a meagre dowry, could not afford to be choosy.

But she wanted Rod!

She became aware that Lord Stewart had taken her hand and was patting it anxiously. "Miss Kilmore, dear lady, I fear I have taken you by surprise, shocked you. Shall I ring for a glass of wine, or your vinaigrette?''

"No, sir, I thank you. I am very well, and most sensible of the honour of your obliging offer." Raising her eyes to his concerned face, she knew she had to give the Marquis of Hazlewood one more opportunity to abandon his prized bachelorhood. "But I fear I must refuse."

"My dear, I wish you will take some time to consider. I am aware that it is a great responsibility. If you wish to make the children's acquaintance before you come to a decision, that is quite understandable and can be arranged without committing you to anything."

"You are very kind, my lord. I do not think I shall change my mind. Pray excuse me. I must speak to my mother."

"Most natural. Allow me to express once more my fervent desire to make you my wife." He kissed her hand and opened the library door, accompanying her into the hall. "I believe I shall go for a ride now. Mr. DeVine has generously invited me to stay at Goff's Acre tonight so as to be able to leave for home early on the morrow. However, if you have not enough time to reconsider my offer before your own departure, you can always inform me by letter."

Under the eyes of the interested footman stationed in the hall, they mounted the stairs together.

Thea paused outside the door of Meg's chamber until she heard Lord Stewart's chamber door click shut as he went to change into riding dress. Then she sped back down the stairs.

"Do you know where Lord Hazlewood is?" she asked the footman.

"His lordship is in Mr. DeVine's study, miss." His expressionless face conveyed as clearly as words his curiosity about such carryings-on among the gentry. No doubt the servants would dub Thea as wayward as Meg after her sister's misbehaviour last night. "Down the right passage, miss," he directed her, "and the second door on the right."

As she hurried down the corridor, she tried to plan exactly what she would say. She would ask for his advice, but what she really wanted was for him to cry, "You can't marry Stewart, because I want to marry you."

Second door on the right. She knocked.

"Come in." It was Will's voice, full of gloom.

She opened the door. Both Will and Roderick were slouched in their chairs, their feet on the desk. When they saw her they hastily lowered their legs and jumped up.

"I beg your pardon," she said, "I do not mean to interrupt. I just wanted a word with Lord Hazlewood, but it can wait."

"Not at all," said her host courteously, waving her to his chair. "I was thinking of going for a ride." He trudged out, even his gait expressive of dejection.

Too agitated to sit down, Thea passed the chair and stopped before a bookshelf. She found herself facing such titles as *A Short Essay on Agricultural Improvements* and *Observations on the Barrenness of Fruit-Trees*. She took down the latter and flipped through it blindly.

"I'm sure Will would be happy to lend it to you." Roderick's amused voice came from close behind her.

With a gasp, she shook her head and pushed the book back between its companions.

"Are you come to plead Miss Megan's case?" He smiled as she turned to him. "I have already put in a good word, you know. She was simply misled by youthful exuberance."

"Yes. Thank you. No." She made a gesture of hopeless confusion.

He caught her hands in his. "What is it, Thea?"

"Lord Stewart has asked me to be his wife."

Dropping her hands, he swung away to lean heavily with both fists on the desk. "My dear Miss Kilmore, I cannot possibly advise you. You must do as you see fit."

She stared blankly at his back. His anger would be preferable to the coldness in his voice. Shivering, she slipped past him and fled up to her chamber.

With relief she recalled that he was not to drive her back to Town. She needed time to regain her composure before she would be able to face Rod again.

CHAPTER EIGHTEEN

UNLIKE THEA'S MISERY, Meg's gloom was of brief duration. By the sixth day of January, her resilient spirits were restored to their usual exuberance.

"Is it not a splendid notion to perform *Twelfth Night* on Twelfth Night?" She waltzed around the drawing-room with an imaginary partner, her skirts swirling. Her gown was of palest pink *crêpe lisse,* with wild roses in a slightly darker pink set on around the hem, some in bud, some open to show a circlet of gold stamens.

"You are merry as a cricket," said Penny drily, her knitting needles clicking away.

"He is willing to forgive me." She stopped before Thea and sank in a deep curtsy. "Do you not think he is willing to forgive me? Lady Lewin invited us both to the theatre before...before that night, but he could have found an excuse to cry off. Could he not, Mama?"

"I daresay," said the dowager, smiling. "He is a gentleman of considerable address."

"I shall dazzle him," said Meg, twirling again, "and not spare a single glance for any other gentleman." She paused by the window and peeped out. "Oh, here is the Lewins' carriage come to fetch me."

"Come, then, darling." The dowager folded her embroidery and set it aside. "I shall see you off. I want to be sure your abigail understands that she is to wait for you at the Lewins'."

They went out.

"I hope she is right," said Thea. "How odd it will seem to see my little sister wed."

"Do you regret having refused Lord Stewart?" Penny asked.

"No. Especially since we heard that he is already betrothed to an impoverished widow with two daughters! I might have regretted it, simply for the sake of his children, if he had offered for Mrs. Wilmington, but this Mrs. Philpots sounds ideal for him."

"True, but seriously, do you not wish to be married?"

Thea sighed. "Before you came to Newkirk, I held the lowest opinion of marriage. My parents did not precisely provide an example of domestic felicity! Seeing you and Jason so happy has changed my view. I should like to be wed, but not to a man I do not love and who does not love me."

"Forgive me, Thea dear, if I am wrong, but I believe you have already given your heart—to Lord Hazlewood. Will you not tell me what is wrong? You restored harmony between Jason and me, and I cannot remain aloof when you are unhappy."

"He has only called once since we came home, and that such a short, formal visit!" Her voice wavered. "Oh, Penny, I told him Lord Stewart asked for my hand, thinking that if he loved me he would advise me to refuse, even insist that I refuse. But he just told me coldly to make up my own mind. He doesn't love me. He only befriended me because he is a gallant gentleman and I needed his aid."

"My dear, I cannot answer for his feelings, but how could he possibly guess that you care for him when you led him to believe you were considering an offer from another man?''

Thea winced. "I have been as caper-witted as Meg, have I not? I did see a parallel with her behaviour, before I went to him, but I rushed on without reflection. What shall I do?''

"For a start, make sure he is aware that you rejected Lord Stewart.''

"Yes, of course. But I cannot be so forward as to tell him that I love him unless he gives some sign of reciprocating my feelings.''

"No, it would be shockingly vulgar to set your cap at him," Penny agreed, "and quite dreadful if he gave you a set-down. Let me think. Suppose you were to—''

"Oh, hush, Mama is coming back.''

Jason came in with his mother. "I'm away," he said, bending over the back of Penny's chair and putting his arms around her, "if you are sure you don't mind, love?''

"A fine thing it would be if I were to stop you going to meet Lord Hazlewood, when he has so kindly agreed to advise you on finding a good bailiff!''

"I only wish he had accepted my invitation to dine here, but he was already engaged for dinner. He chose Brooks's because he is to meet someone else there later, I collect. He is a busy man and I must find a factor soon. I shall not be long gone, not more than a couple of hours.'' He leaned down to kiss Penny's cheek, waved a farewell to his mother and sister, and departed.

"Drat," said Penny, "I've dropped three stitches.''

ROD WAS AGREEABLY impressed by Jason Kilmore's serious intention of improving his estate. He had always considered the baron a fribble, his determination to buy back the farms his father had sold nothing more than a matter of pride. Though they had spent ten days in the same house, he had had little to do with the fellow, being occupied in courting Thea.

Like his own, Will's courtship had ended in disaster, but before that, apparently, he had shown Kilmore around the Goff's Acre farms. Kilmore had been impressed enough to ask advice about hiring a bailiff, and Will—damn his eyes!—had referred him to his cousin. Hence this reluctant meeting in the reading-room at his club.

"I only hope poor old Bodger doesn't take his enforced retirement to heart," Kilmore said now, surprising Rod yet again. Who would have thought the man sensitive enough to be concerned over his present bailiff's feelings?

"From what you have said, I suspect he will be relieved," said Rod. "For whatever reasons, he has had little experience ..." Pausing, he nodded to the waiter who had come up to them bearing a silver salver.

With a frown, Kilmore took the proffered letter. "You'll excuse me if I read it at once, Hazlewood? My wife ..." His frown deepened as he read the superscription. He broke the seal with an abrupt gesture and perused the note. Suddenly pale, he jumped to his feet. "Hell and damnation!"

"I trust Lady Kilmore is not taken ill?"

"Taken hostage!" He groaned. "If he has hurt her, I'll kill the ruffian! Five thousand pounds! Where am I to find five thousand pounds at this time of night?" He dropped back into his chair and sank his head in his hands. "Oh Penny, Penny, if he has hurt you!"

"Her uncle?"

"Yes." Kilmore started up again. Pacing and gesturing wildly, he raised his voice to a near shout. "I shall kill him, I swear it. I should have done it long ago." He swung to face Rod. "Lend me five thousand."

Everyone in the room was staring. Rod deplored his companion's loss of self-control and his resulting inability to think straight. "Sit down," he said sharply. "Don't be a numbskull. What would you do with five thousand pounds? Give it to Vaughn and he'll come back later for more. If you intend to kill him, there's no earthly reason to pay him first, though it's not a course of action I can advise. You would certainly be convicted of manslaughter, if not murder."

"What am I to do?"

"Let me see the letter." The scrawled message was easy enough to decipher:

I have your wife. Bring £5,000 to 3, Chapel Court, Swallow Street, by midnight. Come alone if you want to see her again alive.

Too short a time to lay plans. Having met Vaughn, Rod had no confidence in the fellow's ability to keep his temper if Kilmore were not there by midnight. To kill his niece would avail him nothing, but one could not rely upon him to let that restrain his violence. "Let's go. It can't be more than half a mile. It will be quicker to walk than to send for a carriage."

The distraught husband was not to be held to a walk, nor even a rapid stride. They ran along Piccadilly to Swallow Street. As it was in process of being transformed into Regent Street, a grand approach to Regent's Park, that narrow thoroughfare was lined with rubble. Reflected from a low overcast, the gas lights of the respectable streets to the west provided just enough illumination to prevent Rod and Jason from breaking their necks. Stumbling, steadying each other, they sped northward.

At the corner of Swallow Street and Chapel Court was a heap of broken bricks, sprouting here and there a splintered beam. Looming over it, a blank wall towered: the end of the Chapel Court tenement. The terrace of three tall, narrow dwellings, fronting directly onto the short street, stood dark, dilapidated, derelict, ready for demolition.

Only the nearest showed any sign of life, a faint glow of light in one ground-floor window. A need for caution at last dawned on Jason Kilmore and he crept towards it while Rod gently tried the front door. It was on the latch.

One corner of the sackcloth draping the inside of the window was torn. For what seemed an age, Kilmore peered through the gap, then he pressed his ear to the pane for two or three minutes. He shook his head and stepped back to let Rod look.

Vaughn sat on a broken chair at a rickety table. Before him stood writing materials and a bottle. He was raising to his lips a tumbler of a clear liquid, doubtless gin. Light from an ill-trimmed oil lamp flickered on his unshaven chin, his broken-veined nose. His brown coat was threadbare and a limp blue muffler enveloped his neck. In the few weeks since Rod had last seen him, his appearance had deteriorated from that of a respectable-looking tradesman to a back-slum bully.

Two empty chairs stood at the table. What little Rod could see of the rest of the room was bare, with mildew stains on the walls, broken glass and yellowed newspapers roughly swept into a corner.

Kilmore tugged on his sleeve and they retreated.

"I can scarce believe it is the same man," the baron whispered. "The one time I saw him before, he looked like a prosperous man of business, though he behaved like a brute."

"When I saw him, he was somewhere between the two."

"*You* saw him?" Kilmore asked, incredulous. "When?"

"So the ladies never did tell you? I am surprised that they managed to keep the secret. Vaughn came to your house, and I arrived just in time to prevent him from attacking your elder sister."

"You are very busy about my affairs, my lord! It seems you know more of my household than I."

"Come, this is no time for quarrels, nor for explanations. As far as I could see, Lady Kilmore is not in that room. I suggest we reconnoitre to find where they are holding her. We'd best look round the back."

Stealthy as alley cats, if less silent, they climbed the piles of debris, an exercise that would doubtless cause their respective valets a good deal of grief. Rod bit back an expletive as his knee met a protruding plank. He heard cloth rip.

"Hell and damnation," muttered Kilmore, encountering his own obstacles.

Like the front, the rear of the house was illumined by a single glowing rectangle. The window was better covered, however. Try as they might, they could see nothing in the room beyond it. Kilmore tried the door next to it.

"Not locked. I'm going in," he said grimly. "Penny must be in there. I can't let her suffer alone any longer."

"If Vaughn is in his senses, he won't have her here."

"Then I shall beat her whereabouts out of him. I've floored him before, and I'll floor him again."

"He probably has accomplices," Rod warned. "We need more information before rushing in."

"He has my wife," the baron snarled. "That's all the information I need. Are you with me or not?"

"Very well, but if there are others, at least let us divide their attention. Both doors are unlocked. You take the rear, I'll go around to the front, and we'll break in at the same moment. Give me ten minutes—no, better make it fifteen, considering what's in the way. It's only twenty past eleven." By the dim light from the window, they synchronized their watches.

Rod scrambled back round to Chapel Court. Checking his watch, he found he had overestimated the time he needed. Ten minutes to wait.

Watch in hand, he leaned against the wall. Too late to worry about damage to his coat. The seconds ticked past. Somewhere not far off a horse plodded by, the slow rhythm of its hooves sounding weary. One minute. Two minutes.

He heard a distant cry. Amazing how quiet these streets were at this time of night.

And then came a thud within the room behind him. He applied his eye to the gap in the sackcloth just in time to see two bruisers drag in Kilmore's limp body.

"Jus' like you said, guv, he crep' in the back way and looked in the room and there we was waiting."

Rod gritted his teeth. *Damn the man!* The baron had lost his composure, lost his prudence, lost his patience, and ruined their chance of success. Alone, Rod could not possibly take on those three brutes at once, for all his size and expertise.

The sensible course would be to go for help. But now that Vaughn had both Kilmores in his power, who could guess what he was planning? He'd be furious when he discovered Kilmore had brought no ransom. Given his temper, he was likely to put the present satisfaction of revenge higher than the hope of money in the future.

The only chance was to rescue Lady Kilmore before Vaughn stopped gloating over her husband's capture. Rod had to get into the house and search for her. Slipping and sliding in his haste, he clambered back towards the rear.

He would never forgive himself, and Thea would never forgive him, if Lady Kilmore came to harm. Where the devil was she?

CHAPTER NINETEEN

PENNY CAST OFF her knitting and smoothed the tiny yellow jacket on her lap with a sigh of satisfaction. She looked up as Thea's quiet voice stopped.

"You read so well," she said, "and Mr. Wordsworth's poems are so soothing the words just flow past one like a mountain stream. Shall I ring for tea? Your throat is dry, I daresay."

"A little. Don't get up, Penny, I'll ring." Thea went to the bell-pull. "How is your fringe coming, Mama?"

The dowager stared in dismay at the yards of fringe strewn about her ankles. "Oh dear, I have knotted far too much. I was listening to your reading, dear, instead of watching what I was doing."

"We shall find a use for it, never fear," said Penny, laughing. The butler entered and she went on, "Dunmow, the tea tray, if you please. Bring five cups—his lordship and Miss Megan should be back at any moment—and some of the Twelfth Cake."

"Yes, my lady." The butler went out.

"I thought Jason would be back by now," Thea said, helping her mother wind the fringe onto a card. "Oh, there is the doorbell now. Either Meg is home or Jason has mislaid his key."

Dunmow reappeared, silver salver in hand. "A letter, my lady." His disapproval of those who delivered messages so late in the evening was plain to see.

Penny took it, looked at it, and turned pale. "Uncle Vaughn's hand," she whispered.

Heart in throat, Thea was at her side in a flash. Kneeling by her chair, she put her arm about her sister-in-law's shoulders. "Are you certain?" she asked, though she had little doubt.

"Yes. Will you read it, Thea?"

She scanned it quickly before reading it aloud. No way to soften the message occurred to her. "Your husband is in my hands." Her voice shook. "If you want to see him alive, bring £5,000 to 3, Chapel Court, Swallow Street, by midnight. Come alone."

Penny sank back, her eyes closed. "He must be drunk to think I have so much money to hand, or can get it at this time of night!" She sat up. "My jewels! They are not worth so much, but perhaps they will satisfy him for now. Dunmow, have Nancy bring down my jewels, and whatever of the ready is available, and my outdoor clothes. Quickly!"

"Wait!" said Thea. "You cannot possibly go, Penny. Think of the child! We must send for the marquis, or rather inform him and beg his help, since it would waste time for him to come here. Whether Jason was abducted on the way to Brooks's or after he left, Lord Hazlewood is probably still there. Dunmow, paper and pen."

The butler disappeared like a pellet from a popgun and reappeared as abruptly with writing materials. "Here, miss. I'll send George to the mews to have a horse saddled ready, and Geoffrey can run after with your letter soon as it's wrote. He'll have to go on to Arlington Street if his lordship isn't at the club. Then, meantimes, Mrs. Nancy can get together the needful and I'll have the carriage brought round, just in case."

"Yes, well thought of, Dunmow," Thea agreed, writing as she listened. As he vanished again, shouting for George, she read what she had written. "My dear Roderick... Your most affectionate..." Oh, Lord! No time to do it over. Whatever his opinion of her, surely her knight would ride to the rescue one more time? She blotted the ink, folded Mr. Vaughn's note inside, and sealed the paper.

Geoffrey dashed in, his face, scarlet with excitement, clashing with the maroon facings of his blue livery. "I'll gallop all the way, miss," he promised.

"And gallop back," she said softly. "If you cannot find Lord Hazlewood, I shall go in her ladyship's place."

"You're a right Trojan, miss," he blurted out, and dashed off with the note.

Thea turned her attention back to Penny and her mother. The dowager bent over her daughter-in-law, urging her to go upstairs and lie down.

"I cannot," Penny said faintly, her hand pressed to her abdomen. "Geoffrey may not find the marquis. Even if he does, Hazlewood may not be able to help. I cannot leave Jason to my uncle's mercy. He has none."

"Mama, she *must* not go. If necessary, I shall go in your place, Penny. Jason is my brother. I am as tall as you, and if I wear your Russian cloak with the hood raised, Mr. Vaughn will not know the difference. Besides, what can it matter to him who brings the money?"

"Less money than he has demanded. Besides, I fear he wants revenge as much as the ready."

Nancy came in, bearing the sable-trimmed cloak, a leather jewellery case, and a purse. The thin, grey-haired woman took one look at her mistress and set down her burdens with a thud. "I brought everything, but it's straight to bed with you, Miss Penny. You're not going anywheres in your condition, and I'll have no argufying, if you please."

Penny did not give in so easily. The persuasions of her maid, her mother-in-law, and Thea might never have convinced her, but suddenly in the middle of the debate, she clutched her middle with both hands.

"It's moving," she said in a strange voice.

After that, she agreed to recline on a sofa. As she lay back, all joy at the baby's quickening destroyed by its father's peril, Dunmow came in.

"The carriage is at the door, my lady."

They all stared at one another in silence, and then at the clock on the mantel. "If Geoffrey is not back in fifteen minutes," said Thea, her voice as odd as Penny's, "I shall leave anyway, or I may be too late."

Her mother burst into tears. Realizing she was torn between terror for her son, for her daughter, and for her grandchild, Thea hugged her. Over her head, she caught Penny's desperate, pleading gaze, silently begging forgiveness. And then they all heard the front door open and close.

Meg rushed in, radiant, tugging Mr. DeVine after her by the hand. "Mama, Thea, Penny," she cried, "we are engaged to be married! Will says..." Her words trailed away as she took in the scene before her. She put her hand to her mouth, her eyes wide with alarm.

"Lady Kilmore, what is wrong?" asked Will sharply, pulling Meg to him and slipping his arm about her waist with a lack of decorum that was endearing in one usually so proper.

Penny and Thea had scarce finished explaining when Geoffrey burst into the drawing-room, red now with exertion as well as excitement. Behind him surged George and a youth and a small boy, the last two in Hazlewood olive green livery. Under Dunmow's glare they all sprang to attention.

"Begging your ladyship's pardon," Geoffrey began, "Lord Hazlewood weren't at his club nor at home, but me and George'll go with Miss Thea and we'll do for that villain proper, you see if we don't. This here's Peter, his lordship's tiger, and Billy, the laddy as was his tiger. They wants to go too, being as they knows Miss Thea, like."

"Splendid fellows," said Will, taking charge. "Dunmow, are there any pistols in the house?"

Jason's duelling pistols being locked up, Dunmow produced a horse-pistol, which Will appropriated, and a shotgun. The latter he rejected, since none of the men had ever fired one. He armed them with pokers.

"You must stay and guard the rest of the ladies," he told the butler. "No, Meg, er, Miss Megan, you can't come."

Meg pouted, but quickly yielded. The reason soon became apparent: just as Scargill set the carriage in motion she opened the door and sprang in. It was too late to stop and send her home.

"I have come to chaperon my sister," she said pertly, settling beside Will.

"Then go and sit next to her," he ordered, then spoiled his sternness by adding, "I cannot think with you beside me."

"I trust that is intended as a compliment," she exclaimed, laughing, but she obeyed. She soon lost her cheerfulness when they started to make plans.

Will was all for leaving both young ladies outside and rushing the house with the footmen. "If I had thought before," he said, "you need not have come at all, Miss Kilmore."

For a moment Thea hoped that the terrifying task before her was unnecessary. "No, that would endanger Jason," she pointed out reluctantly, "particularly if Mr. Vaughn has accomplices. He...he may be unable to join in the fight."

"Hurt?" whispered Meg.

"More likely tied up." Will leaned across to pat her hand. "A good point, Miss Kilmore. What do you suggest?"

"I shall just go in and attempt to buy his release." The jewellery case and purse lay beside her on the seat. "Mr. Vaughn may well let us go. If not... well, at least I can distract his attention while you break in."

"While the others break in," he corrected. "I shall accompany you."

"No. He said Penny was to go alone." Alone. She reached for Meg's hand, glad her little sister had come. Suddenly Thea was very, very frightened. Will seemed so slight and young, too easily overruled. If only Roderick were here!

The rest of the brief journey passed in a daze. Approaching via King Street, the carriage stopped on the corner of Chapel Court. Will helped Thea down and turned to Meg.

She put her word in first. "*Please*, Will, let me come. I *promise* I shall not enter the house until you tell me it is safe, but if you or Thea or Jason is hurt, I *must* be there to help."

Her earnest plea won him over. With a lady on either arm, followed by three footmen and a tiger, he proceeded up the dark street as if on a morning stroll in Bond Street.

All too soon, Mr. DeVine removed his supporting arms and applied his eye to a chink of light at one corner of a ground-floor window. Thea and Meg clung together at a cautious distance, guarded by George, Geoffrey, Billy, and Peter, all bursting with silent excitement. After a moment Will returned to them.

"Kilmore's there all right," he reported in a grim undertone. "He's tied to a chair, and he's been . . . and there are at least two ruffians in the room. You go in, Miss Kilmore. I feel much better about this whole business since I'll be able to see what's going on."

Thea appreciated the reason for his optimism, but as she approached the door and he turned to give his troops their orders, she felt utterly deserted.

The man who answered her knock was no more than a hulking shadow. "So 'ere's 'er ladyship," he said mockingly. His breath was foul, his voice uneducated, not Mr. Vaughn's. He grasped her wrist to draw her into the dark hall.

She winced at the rough handling and dropped the purse. It landed with a clink of coins. The man swiftly stooped to retrieve it. Thea wished she had provided herself with a poker, the more so when he next seized the jewellery case from her other hand. He glanced at the open front door, then slammed it.

"Nah," he said with regret, "Vaughn's got a nasty way wiv 'im when 'e's miffed." The case under one beefy arm, he grabbed her again and hustled her through the nearest door.

Vaguely aware of another ruffian moving in behind her, she found herself face to face with Mr. Vaughn. Hastily she dropped her head, which was covered by the cloak's hood. Not only was he an alarming and repellent sight, but she did not want him to guess she was not his niece.

For the moment he ignored her, interested as he was in the purse and case the first man dropped on the table in front of him. He pushed aside his bottle, glass, and inkstand. "What's she brought, cully?"

With greedy fingers he opened the case while his henchman emptied the purse. The man behind Thea rushed forward to catch a gleaming guinea that rolled onto the floor.

Vaughn's dirty fingers pawed through Penny's jewels. "Nice," he sneered, looking up, "but these ain't worth five thousand. What else have you got for me?"

"Nothing," Thea said in a low voice. "That is the best I could do tonight. Surely it is sufficient. Let us go."

"Let you go?" His laugh was drunkenly malicious. "You must be roasting me, Niece. You and hubby here have forced me to go to a lot of trouble, and I'm going to make you sorry for it."

At last Thea raised her head. "But I am not..." She gasped as she saw Jason in the corner beyond him. Tied to a chair, as Will had said... From the corner of his mouth, gagged with a dirty rag, blood trickled down his chin, and another trickle descended his temple from a damp, matted patch of dark hair. One eye was swollen shut; the other regarded her with an urgent message she could not read. "I am not your niece, Mr. Vaughn," Thea finished firmly. "I am Lord Kilmore's sister."

From the open door behind her came a roar of rage. A huge, wild figure in dilapidated evening dress stormed past her, shoving her aside. The large and furious gentleman cracked together the heads of two surprised villains. As they sank, dazed, to the floor, he sent Mr.

Vaughn flying from his chair with a superb uppercut to the jaw. And then he rounded on Thea.

"What the devil do you think you're doing," he shouted, advancing on her, his face flushed with wrath, "throwing yourself in danger's way like the veriest feather-brained ninnyhammer? How dare you interfere! Damn it, have you no faith in me? I've a deuced good mind to—"

What he had a good mind to do, Thea never discovered. Another discovery intervened. Roderick DeVine, Marquis of Hazlewood, the coolest, calmest, most unexcitable gentleman of the beau monde, had lost his temper—had lost his temper at *her*. She could think of only one possible reason.

And so she silenced his tirade with a kiss, a shameless, brazen, arms-around-the-neck-and-hold-on-tight kiss...a kiss that continued, though the small room suddenly filled with people.

A kiss that continued though Thea suddenly came to her senses and realized her shockingly improper behaviour. By then, Roderick's arms were around her, and she couldn't have escaped if she had wanted to, which she did not.

"Well, I must say," Meg declared, "I do think *you* might have kissed *me* like that, Will."

"I shall," he promised, "but not just now. You didn't leave us much to do, coz."

He looked round with pardonable satisfaction. Pokers poised, George, Geoffrey, and Billy had each taken a seat on a recumbent ruffian. Little Peter was playing lookout at the door. Meg was ministering to her brother with spit and a miniscule lace-edged handkerchief. Will lowered his horse-pistol.

Roderick released Thea just enough for her to catch her breath. Gazing down at her with a bemused expression, he said, "There are far too many people about."

"I'd be delighted to depart," Jason, finally able to speak again, said drily. "Penny must be in high fidgets."

One arm still holding Thea close, Rod reached in his pocket and tossed a penknife to his cousin. Meg took a pair of tiny embroidery scissors from her reticule. She and Will attacked Jason's bonds.

The marquis frowned. "Far too slow," he observed. Taking Thea's hand, he led her from the room.

They found a seat of sorts on the lower steps of a narrow staircase. Locked in her beloved's arms, Thea would not have exchanged those stairs for a queen's throne. His strength, his gentleness, his understanding enveloped her, and a tender yet ardent passion astonishing in so self-controlled a gentleman. Now they had no need for words.

All too soon the sweet embrace was interrupted. Will appeared before them waving a sheet of paper and a quill.

"Sign this, will you, coz. Your tiger won't go near Bow Street without your name to it."

Reluctantly, Roderick let go of Thea, signed the paper, and handed it back. Will beckoned Peter over and sent him off.

"The footmen will take care of those miscreants until the constables arrive. I must take Meg home—her mother will be in a tweak. You may congratulate me, Rod. She's accepted me. Meg, that is, not the dowager."

"Congratulations," the marquis muttered, burying his face in Thea's hair, one hand stroking the back of her neck, sending shivers down her spine.

"I take it you don't want to come? Someone ought to stay till Vaughn and the others are safely under lock and key, but if Miss Kilmore wishes—"

"Devil take it, go away!" bellowed Lord Hazlewood, sorely tried.

Will's grin flashed white in the shadows. "I'll send the carriage back," he promised.

At that moment Meg supported her limping brother into the hall. "By the way, Hazlewood," said Jason sardonically, "you have my permission to address my sister." The three departed into the night.

Roderick nibbled thoughtfully on Thea's ear. "I could go down on my knees," he offered, "but I should have to remove you from them first."

"Pray don't." She snuggled closer, or would have had it been possible.

"I could make a speech," he offered, "but it would be a shocking waste of time."

"Pray don't." After tonight, they would have to behave with propriety and circumspection until... until—

"Will you marry me?"

"Oh yes, Rod." She sighed contentedly. "I should like it of all things."

The constables, bursting in half an hour later, were positively scandalized at the goings-on among the nobs.

WHO SAYS THE PAST IS OLD NEWS?

Harlequin Regency Romance is bringing the past to life with six exciting new books!

June marks the publication of our 100th title and an all-new concept. The REGENCY QUARTET brings you a collection of stories by well-known British authors, offering you hours of big-book enjoyment. And you'll be sure to fall in love with a simply divine comedy, A MATCH MADE IN HEAVEN, by reader favorite Jeanne Carmichael. And don't miss the latest from popular author Barbara Neil—GENTLEMAN ROGUE.

Feel the heat in July and August with sizzling Regency romances by Barbara Neil, Elizabeth Michaels, Winifred Witton and Brenda Hiatt.

Join us this summer and find out what's new!

Look for Harlequin Regency Romance wherever Harlequin books are sold.

Harlequin is proud to present our best authors and their best books. Always the best for your reading pleasure!

Throughout 1993, Harlequin will bring you exciting books by some of the top names in contemporary romance!

In June, look for *Threats and Promises* by

The plan was to make her nervous....

Lauren Stevens was so preoccupied with her new looks and her new business that she really didn't notice a pattern to the peculiar "little incidents"—incidents that could eventually take her life. However, she did notice the sudden appearance of the attractive and interesting Matt Kruger who *claimed* to be a close friend of her dead brother....

Find out more in THREATS AND PROMISES ... available wherever Harlequin books are sold.

THREE UNFORGETTABLE HEROINES
THREE AWARD-WINNING AUTHORS

Untamed
MAVERICK HEARTS

A unique collection of historical short stories that
capture the spirit of America's last frontier.

HEATHER GRAHAM POZZESSERE—over 10 million copies
of her books in print worldwide
Lonesome Rider—The story of an Eastern widow and the
renegade half-breed who becomes her protector.

PATRICIA POTTER—an author whose books are consistently
Waldenbooks bestsellers
Against the Wind—Two people, battered by heartache, prove
that love can heal all.

JOAN JOHNSTON—award-winning Western historical author
with 17 books to her credit
One Simple Wish—A woman with a past discovers that
dreams really do come true.

Join us for an exciting journey West with
UNTAMED
Available in July, wherever Harlequin books are sold.

MAV93